GREAT EXPECTATIONS

A Kaplan Vocabulary-Building Classic for Young Readers

**Look for more
Kaplan Vocabulary-Building Classics
for Young Readers**

The Adventures of Tom Sawyer
by Mark Twain

Treasure Island
by Robert Louis Stevenson

Little Women
by Louisa May Alcott

GREAT EXPECTATIONS

A Kaplan Vocabulary-Building Classic for Young Readers

CHARLES DICKENS

ABRIDGED

SIMON & SCHUSTER

NEW YORK   LONDON   SYDNEY   TORONTO

Kaplan Publishing
Published by SIMON & SCHUSTER
1230 Avenue of the Americas
New York, NY 10020

Editorial Director: Jennifer Farthing
Project Editor: Eileen McDonnell
Content Manager: Patrick Kennedy
Abridgement and Adaptation: Caroline Leavitt for Ivy Gate Books
Interior Design: Ismail Soyugenc for Ivy Gate Books
Cover Design: Mark Weaver

Manufactured in the United States of America
Published simultaneously in Canada

10 9 8 7 6 5 4 3 2 1

April 2006
ISBN-13: 978-0-7432-8341-0
ISBN-10:   0-7432-8341-4

For information regarding special discounts for bulk purchases, please contact Simon & Schuster Special Sales at 1-800-456-6798 or business@simonandschuster.com.

TABLE OF CONTENTS

HOW TO USE THIS BOOK

Charles Dickens's *Great Expectations* is a classic tale of a young person's dream to rise out of humble beginnings. It also is a way for young people today to raise their vocabularies – for tests as well as for daily writing and speaking.

Kaplan makes it as easy as 1-2-3 for you to learn dozens – even hundreds – of new words just by reading this classic story. On the right-hand pages you will find the words of Dickens's famous novel. On each page you will find words that have been bolded (put into heavy, dark type). These are words you may be tested on, both in your specific subjects and in standardized tests. On the left-hand pages you'll find information about those words: how to pronounce them, what part of speech they are, what they mean, and even synonyms. In short, you'll find everything you will need to master each of these special words in the story.

Not all of the challenging or unusual words in *Great Expectations* are likely to be found on tests.

Some are words that were used often in Dickens's day, 150 years ago and more, but are uncommon today. Others are words that are specific to nineteenth-century occupations or activities. You might want to learn these words as well, even though they are not likely to be tested. For this reason we have underlined them and put information about them in the glossary at the back of this book.

You'll also find other helpful features in this book. "Charles Dickens and *Great Expectations*" provides useful information about Dickens's life and this particular book, all of which will help you enjoy your reading even more. At the back of the book you will also find discussion questions. These will get you thinking about the characters, events, and meaning of this classic novel. They will also help you get ready to discuss it in class, with friends, or with your family members.

The back of the book also contains a helpful section that will assist you in writing a book report about *Great Expectations*. Use it as an organizer to develop and order your thoughts about the book.

Now that you have found out what is in the book – and how to use it – you can get started reading and enjoying one of the most famous classics of all time.

CHARLES DICKENS AND
GREAT EXPECTATIONS

Charles Dickens was born on February 7, 1812 in England, one of eight children. But he did not have much of a childhood. He was put to work when he was just twelve years old. He had little formal education, yet he taught himself to write and soon was writing for the local newspaper. These stories were published as *The Pickwick Papers,* when Dickens was just 24!

Charles Dickens was known for writing serials. This means he would publish a chapter or two each week. He would always make sure to end each installment with suspense. This would make his readers even more excited and interested to read the next chapter.

Great Expectations was Dickens's thirteenth novel. Dickens originally planned a very different ending, a much sadder one, but his editors worried that readers would not like it, so he changed it and gave his characters hope.

Charles Dickens died on June 9, 1870.

GREAT EXPECTATIONS

INFANT (<u>in</u> fuhnt) *adj.*
   relating to a young child
     Synonym: childish

AUTHORITY (uh <u>thor</u> uh tee) *n.*
   1. the right to do something
     Synonym: power
   2. someone who knows a lot about a particular subject
     Synonym: expert

TOMBSTONE (<u>toom</u> stone) *n.*
   stone marking a grave
     Synonym: gravestone

CHAPTER 1

My father's family name being Pirrip, and my Christian name Philip, my **infant** tongue could make of both names nothing longer or clearer than Pip. So, I called myself Pip and came to be called Pip.

I give Pirrip as my father's family name, on the **authority** of his **tombstone** and my sister, Mrs. Joe Gargery, who married the <u>blacksmith</u>.

Ours was the marsh country, down by the river, twenty miles from the sea. My first most

VIVID (<u>viv</u> id) *adj.*
　　strong or bright
　　　　Synonym: sharp

MEMORY (<u>mem</u> uh ree) *n.*
　　thoughts and images about something that has
　　happened in the past
　　　　Synonyms: remembrance, recollection

BLEAK (bleek) *adj.*
　　bare, cold, empty
　　　　Synonym: barren

RAVENOUSLY (<u>rav</u> uh nuhss lee) *adv.*
　　displaying or having a large appetite
　　　　Synonym: hungrily

vivid memory was on a cold afternoon. I was in the churchyard, a **bleak** place overgrown with weeds. There Philip Pirrip, and Georgiana his wife, and their five infant children were buried. Beyond the churchyard was the river, and beyond the river was the sea. The small bundle of shivers growing afraid of it all and beginning to cry, was Pip.

"Hold your noise!" cried a terrible voice. A man leaped up from among the graves. "Keep still or I'll cut your throat!"

A fearful man, all in gray, with a great iron on his leg, seized me by the chin.

"Don't cut my throat, sir!" I begged in terror.

"Tell us your name!" said the man. "Quick!"

"Pip. Pip, sir."

"Show us where you live," said the man.

I pointed to a mile or more from the church.

The man, after looking at me for a moment, turned me upside down and emptied my pockets. There was noting in them but a piece of bread. He sat me on a high tombstone, trembling while he ate the bread **ravenously**.

TIMIDLY (<u>tim</u> id lee) *adv.*
in an easily frightened way
Synonyms: shyly, fearfully

ATTEND (uh <u>tend</u>) *v.* **-ing, -ed**
1. pay attention to
Synonym: listen
2. to take care of
Synonyms: help, assist

CONCERNING (kuhn <u>surn</u> ing) *prep.*
having to do with
Synonyms: regarding, about

I held tighter, partly to keep myself upon it, partly to keep myself from crying.

Said the man. "Where's your mother?"

"There, sir!" I **timidly** explained, pointing to the graves. "Also my father."

"Ha!" he muttered. "Who d'ye live with?"

"My sister, sir, Mrs. Joe Gargery, wife of Joe Gargery, the blacksmith, sir."

"Blacksmith, eh?" said he. After looking at his leg and me several times, he came closer to my tombstone, took me by both arms, and tilted me back as far as he could hold me.

"You get me a file and <u>wittles</u>. Or I'll have your heart and liver out." He tilted me again.

I was really frightened, and so giddy that I clung to him with both hands. "If you would kindly let me keep upright, I could **attend** more."

"You bring me, tomorrow morning early, that file and them wittles to the Battery. You never dare to say a word or dare to make a sign **concerning** your having seen me and I will let you live. You fail and your heart and your liver will be tore out, roasted, and ate. Now, I ain't

ELUDE (i <u>lood</u>) *v.* **-ing, -ed**
to move away from
Synonyms: avoid, escape, get away,
slip by

REPUTATION (rep yuh <u>tay</u> shuhn) *n.*
someone's worth as judged by other people
Synonyms: character, report, note

alone. There's a young man hid with me. I am keeping that young man from harming you with great difficulty. Now, what do you say?"

I said that I would get him the file, and I would get him what food I could, and I would come to him early in the morning.

"Now," he went on, "you get home!"

He hugged his body in both his arms and limped towards the low church wall. As I saw him go, picking his way among the nettles, he looked as if he were **eluding** the hands of the dead people, stretching up out of their graves to pull him in.

When he came to the low church wall, he turned around to look for me. When I saw him turning, I set my face towards home, and made the best use of my legs.

The marshes were just a long black line. I ran home without stopping.

My sister, Mrs. Joe Gargery, was more than twenty years older than I and had a **reputation** with the neigbors because she had brought me up "by hand." She had a hard and heavy

FLAXEN (<u>flaks</u> uhn) *adj.*
    yellow
        Synonym: golden

CONFIDENCE (<u>kon</u> fuh denss) *n.*
    information that is kept private
        Synonym: secret

IMPART (im <u>part</u>) *v.* **-ing**, **-ed**
    to pass on, to give something to someone
        Synonyms: tell, show, convey

LATCH (lach) *n.*
    a fastener for a door
        Synonym: lock

hand, and was much in the habit of laying it upon her husband as well as upon me.

Joe was a fair man, with **flaxen** curls. He was a good-natured fellow, a sort of Hercules in strength, and also in weakness.

My sister, Mrs. Joe, with black hair and eyes, was tall and bony, and almost always wore a coarse apron.

Joe's <u>forge</u> was connected to our house, which was a wooden house. When I ran home from the churchyard, the forge was shut up, and Joe was sitting alone in the kitchen. Joe and I being fellow sufferers, and having **confidences** as such, Joe **imparted** a warning to me, the moment I raised the **latch** of the door.

"Mrs. Joe has been out a dozen times, looking for you, Pip. And she's got Tickler with her."

Tickler was a wax-ended piece of cane, worn smooth by contact with my tickled frame.

"Pip. She's a-coming! Get behind the door!"

I took the advice. My sister, Mrs. Joe, throwing the door wide open, and finding me behind it, hit me with Tickler.

FUGITIVE (<u>fyoo</u> juh tiv) *n.*
someone on the run from the law
Synonym: escapee

LARCENY (<u>lar</u> se nee) *n.*
an act of theft
Synonyms: thievery, robbery

RESERVE (ri <u>zurve</u>) *n.*
an amount held back for future use
Synonyms: savings, store, hoard, supply

ACQUAINTANCE (uh <u>kwayn</u> tuhnss) *n.*
someone known but not very well
Synonyms: contact, associate

GUILTY (<u>gil</u> tee) *adj.*
feeling badly for doing something wrong
Synonyms: ashamed, culpable

ERRAND (<u>er</u> uhnd) *n.*
a job of picking up or delivering something
Synonyms: job, task

"Where have you been, you young monkey?" said Mrs. Joe, stamping her foot.

"I have only been to the churchyard," said I, crying.

"Churchyard!" repeated my sister.

I looked at the fire. The **fugitive** out on the marshes with the ironed leg, the mysterious young man, the file, the food, and the **larceny** I was to do rose before me in the coals.

My sister cut bread and butter for us. I was hungry, but I dared not eat my slice. I must have something in **reserve** for my dreadful **acquaintance** and the still more dreadful young man. I put my bread and butter down the leg of my trousers.

I felt **guilty** that I was going to rob Mrs. Joe – I never thought I was going to rob Joe, for I never thought of any of the housekeeping property as his. I kept one hand on my bread and butter as I sat or when I was ordered about the kitchen on any **errand**. It almost drove me out of my mind. Then I thought I heard the voice outside of the man with the iron on his leg. If ever anybody's hair stood on end with terror, mine must have done so then.

DEPOSIT (di <u>poz</u> it) *v.* **-ing**, **-ed**
to lay down or put something somewhere
Synonyms: place, situate

DESPERATION (dess pur <u>ay</u> shun) *n.*
a feeling that you will do anything to change a situation
Synonyms: hopelessness, fear

It was Christmas Eve, and I had to stir the pudding for the next day. I found it hard to work having the bread and butter hidden at my ankle. I slipped away and **deposited** the food in my bedroom.

"Oh!" said I, hearing a great noise, "was that great guns, Joe?"

"Ah!" said Joe. "There was a convict who escaped last night. And they fired a warning shot to him. And now they're firing another."

Said I, "I should like to know where the firing comes from?"

Exclaimed my sister, "From the Hulks! Hulks are prison-ships!"

"I wonder who's put into prison-ships, and why they're put there?" said I, with quiet **desperation**.

Mrs. Joe rose. "People are put in the Hulks because they murder and rob and do all sorts of bad, and they always begin by asking questions. Now, you get along to bed!"

I went upstairs in the dark, worrying greatly about the Hulks and how close to me they were. I was clearly on my way there. I had begun by

MORTAL (<u>mor</u> tuhl) *adj.*
  so intense that it seems like death
    Synonyms: deadly, fatal

EXTRACT (ex <u>trakt</u>) *v.* **-ing**, **-ed**
  to pull out or pull away
    Synonym: remove

DIKE (dike) *n.*
  a high wall that blocks water
    Synonym: dam

asking questions, and now I was going to rob Mrs. Joe.

I was in **mortal** terror of the young man who wanted my heart and liver. I was in mortal terror of the convict with the iron leg. I was in mortal terror of myself, from whom an awful promise had been **extracted**. I had no hope of deliverance through my sister.

If I slept at all that night, it was only to imagine myself drifting down the river to the Hulks, a ghostly pirate calling out to me that I had better be hanged at once. I was afraid to sleep for I knew that in the morning I must rob the cupboard.

As soon as it was morning, I got up and went downstairs. I stole some bread, cheese, meat, a meat bone, and a beautiful round pork pie.

There was a door in the kitchen. I unlocked that door and got a file from among Joe's tools. Then I ran for the misty marshes.

The mist was heavier when I got upon the marshes. The gates and **dikes** and banks came bursting at me through the mist, as if they cried

DITCH (ditch) *n.*
    a long, narrow hole dug in the ground
        Synonym: trench

COARSE (korss) *adj.*
    lacking in refinement or polish
        Synonyms: rough, rude

OATH (ohth) *n.*
    1. a swear word
        Synonym: curse
    2. a serious promise
        Synonym: pledge

DECEIVING (dee <u>seev</u> ing) *adj.*
    using trickery or lies
        Synonyms: dishonest, untrustworthy

IMP (imp) *n.*
    a mischievous person
        Synonyms: trouble-maker, scamp

as plainly as could be, "A boy with somebody's else's pork pie! Stop him!"

I had just crossed a **ditch** when I saw the man sitting. I touched him on the shoulder, and he jumped up. It was another man!

And yet this man was dressed in **coarse** gray, too, and had a great iron on his leg, and had a flat felt hat on. He swore an **oath** at me, made a hit at me, and then he ran into the mist, and I lost him.

"It's the young man!" I thought.

I was soon at the Battery after that, and there was the right man, hugging himself and limping, waiting for me. I opened the bundle and emptied my pockets.

He stuffed <u>mincemeat</u> down his throat in a hurry. Then he gobbled bread, cheese, and pork pie, all at once, staring while he did so at the mist all round us, often stopping to listen. "You're not a **deceiving imp**?" he asked. "You brought no one with you?"

"No, sir! No!"

"Well," said he, "I believe you. You'd be but a fierce young hound indeed, if you would help

WRETCHED (<u>rech</u> id) *adj.*
deserving of pity
Synonyms: unfortunate, pitiful, pathetic

SMEAR (smihr) *v.* **-ing**, **-ed**
to blur over a surface
Synonyms: rub, spread

DELICATELY (<u>del</u> uh kuht lee) *adv.*
with great care
Synonyms: gently, daintily

to hunt a **wretched** <u>warmint</u> hunted as near death as this poor wretched warmint is!"

Something clicked in his throat. And he **smeared** his ragged rough sleeve over his eyes.

I pitied him and watched him. As he gradually settled down upon the pie, I made bold to say, "I am glad you enjoy it."

"Thankee, my boy. I do."

"I am afraid you won't leave any of it for the young man that was hid with you."

"Him?" he said. "He don't want no wittles."

"I thought he looked as if he did," said I.

He stopped eating and looked at me. "Looked? When? Where?"

"Just now. Over there," said I, pointing. "I found him asleep and thought it was you."

He held me by the collar and stared at me.

"Dressed like you, you know, only with a hat," I explained, trembling, "and – and – I was very anxious to put this **delicately** – "and with the same reason for wanting to borrow a file. Didn't you hear the cannon last night?"

"When a man's alone on these flats, dying of

CRAM (kram) *v.* **-ing**, **-ed**
to shove into a small space
Synonyms: stuff, squeeze

cold and want, he hears nothin' all night but guns firing and voices calling. But this man," he said, "did you notice anything in him?"

"He had a badly bruised face," said I.

"Where is he?" He **crammed** food into his jacket. "I'll get him! If only I didn't have this iron on my leg! Give us hold of the file, boy."

I showed where the mist had covered the other man, but he was down on the grass, filing at his iron like a madman. I thought the best thing I could do was to slip off. And that I did.

DISCOVERY (diss <u>kuh</u> vuh ree) *n.*
something that has been found or uncovered
Synonyms: finding, detection

FESTIVITY (fess <u>tiv</u> uh tee) *n.*
a time for special events and entertainment
Synonyms: party, celebration

REMORSE (ri <u>morss</u>) *n.*
a feeling of having done something wrong
Synonyms: guilt, penitence, self-reproach

CHAPTER 2

I fully expected to find a <u>constable</u> in the kitchen, waiting to take me to the Hulks. But no **discovery** had yet been made of the robbery. Mrs. Joe was busy getting the house ready for the Christmas **festivities**.

The terrors I had felt whenever Mrs. Joe had gone near the pantry were only to be matched by my **remorse** about what my hands had done.

CLERK (klurk) *n.*
   someone who keeps documents or handles
   paperwork
      Synonym: record-keeper

ADJOURN (uh <u>jurn</u>) *v.* **-ing**, **-ed**
   to leave, to break up a meeting or gathering
      Synonyms: leave, go, recess

MISERABLE (<u>miz</u> ur uh buhl) *adj.*
   very sad and hopeless
      Synonyms: unhappy, pathetic

CLUTCH (kluch) *v.* **-ing**, **-ed**
   to hold tightly
      Synonyms: grab, grasp

Mr. Wopsle, the **clerk** at our church, was to dine with us. So were Mr. Hubble the <u>wheelwright</u> and Mrs. Hubble and Uncle Pumblechook.

The dinner hour was at half-past one. Everything was wonderful. And still, not a word from Mrs. Joe of the robbery.

I opened the door for the company, first to Mr. Wopsle, next to Mr. and Mrs. Hubble, and last of all to Uncle Pumblechook.

We dined in the kitchen, and **adjourned** for the nuts and oranges and apples to the living room, which was a change very like Joe's change from his working-clothes to his Sunday dress. My sister was uncommonly lively.

We all ate and drank and talked through the dinner. Among this good company I felt **miserable**.

To make things worse, my sister said to Joe, "We now need clean plates."

I **clutched** the leg of the table. I saw what was coming, and I felt that this time I really was in trouble.

MURMUR (<u>mur</u> mur) *v.* **-ing**, **-ed**
to talk in hushed tones, to mutter or speak
unclearly
Synonyms: whisper, mumble

COMPLIMENT (<u>kom</u> pluh ment) *n.*
a statement of admiration
Synonyms: praise, congratulation

SHRILL (shril) *adj.*
loud and high-pitched in sound
Synonyms: screeching, shrieking

CONFUSION (kon <u>fyoo</u> zhun) *n.*
without order, not understanding
Synonyms: disorder, chaos, disarray

NECESSITATE (nuh <u>sess</u> uh tate) *v.* **-ing**, **-ed**
to have as a requirement
Synonym: need

"You must taste," said my sister, addressing the guests with her best grace, "such a delightful present of Uncle Pumblechook's: a delicious pork pie!"

The whole company **murmured** their **compliments**.

My sister went to get it. I gave a **shrill** yell of terror. I ran for my life. But I ran no farther than the house door, for there I ran into a party of soldiers with their guns! One held out a pair of handcuffs to me, saying, "Here you are, look sharp!"

The soldiers on our doorstep caused the dinner party to rise from table in **confusion**. Mrs. Joe came from the kitchen empty-handed. "Where's the pie?" she cried. When she saw the soldiers, she stopped short and stared.

"Excuse me, ladies and gentleman," said the sergeant, "I want the blacksmith. The lock of one of these handcuffs is broken. As they are wanted for immediate use, will you take a look at them?"

Joe said that the job would **necessitate**

TROOP (troop) *v.* **-ing, -ed**
to move in a group
Synonym: march

AGONY (<u>ag</u> uh nee) *n.*
terrible pain
Synonyms: suffering, distress

APPREHENSION (ap ri <u>hen</u> shun) *n.*
a state of being concerned or fearful
Synonyms: worry, alarm, anxiety

PERCEIVE (per <u>seeve</u>) *v.* **-ing, -ed**
to understand, see, or recognize
Synonym: notice

the lighting of his forge fire, and would take nearer two hours than one. The men came **trooping** into the kitchen and piled their arms in a corner.

I was in an **agony** of **apprehension**. But I began to **perceive** that the handcuffs were not for me, and that everyone had forgotten the lost pie. I collected a little more of my wits.

"How far are you from the marshes?"

"Just a mile," said Mrs. Joe.

"That'll do. We begin to close in upon 'em about dusk."

"Convicts, sergeant?" asked Mr. Wopsle.

"Ay!" said the sergeant, "Two. Anybody here seen anything?"

Everybody, myself excepted, said no. Nobody thought of me.

"Well!" said the sergeant, "they'll find themselves trapped in a circle, I expect, sooner than they count on. Now, blacksmith! If you're ready, his Majesty the King is."

Joe had got his coat and vest and tie off, and his leather apron on, and passed into the forge.

DECLINE (di <u>kline</u>) *v.* **-ing**, **-ed**
to turn something down, to not accept
something
Synonym: refuse

STRICT (strikt) *adj.*
1. kept within narrow confines
Synonyms: stern, severe
2. carefully following a model or example
Synonyms: exact, faithful

TREASONABLY (<u>tree</u> zuhn uh blee) *adv.*
in a manner that goes against a trust or
confidence
Synonyms: disloyally, treacherously

Then Joe began to hammer and clink, and we all looked on.

At last, Joe's job was done. As Joe got on his coat, he gathered courage to ask that some of us should go down with the soldiers and see what came of the hunt. Mr. Pumblechook and Mr. Hubble **declined**, both wanting a pipe and needing to stay with the ladies. But Mr. Wopsle said he would go, if Joe would. Joe said he would take me.

The sergeant left the ladies, and parted from Mr. Pumblechook. His men took their muskets and fell in line. Mr. Wopsle, Joe, and I, received **strict** orders to keep to the back, and to speak no word after we reached the marshes. When we were all out in the cold air and were steadily moving towards our business, I **treasonably** whispered to Joe, "I hope, Joe, we won't find them." And Joe whispered to me, "I'd give anythink if they had run, Pip."

We were stopped a few minutes by a signal from the sergeant's hand, while two or three of his men went among the graves. They came

DREAD (dred) *n.*
a state of worry about future harm
Synonym: fear, anxiety, apprehension

BETRAY (bi <u>tray</u>) *v.* **-ing, -ed**
to be false, to commit treason
Synonym: double-cross

APPARENT (uh <u>pa</u> rent) *adj.*
easily seen, known, or understood
Synonyms: clear, evident

STIFLED (stye <u>fuhld</u>) *adj.*
held back, kept silent
Synonyms: muffled, smothered, suppressed

back to us without finding anything, and then we struck out on the open marshes, through the gate at the side of the churchyard. Now that we were out upon the wilderness, I felt great **dread**. What if we should come upon them? Would my particular convict think that it was I who had brought the soldiers there? Would he believe that I had **betrayed** him?

I looked all about for any sign of the convicts. I could see none, I could hear none. Suddenly, there was a long shout. No, there seemed to be two or more shouts raised together.

It was a run indeed now. Down banks and up banks and over gates and splashing into dikes. As we came nearer to the shouting, it became more and more **apparent** that it was made by more than one voice. After a while, we could hear one voice calling "Murder!" and another voice calling, "This way for the runaway convicts!" Then both voices would sounded **stifled** in a struggle, and then they broke out again. And when it had come to this, the soldiers ran like deer, and Joe too.

SURRENDER (suh <u>ren</u> dur) *v.* **-ing**, **-ed**
to admit you are beaten
Synonyms: give up, yield

PLIGHT (plite) *n.*
a difficult situation
Synonyms: predicament, dilemma

LIVID (<u>liv</u> ud) *adj.*
filled with emotion, terribly angry
Synonyms: furious, upset

The sergeant ran in first.

"Here are both men!" panted the sergeant, struggling at the bottom of a ditch. "**Surrender**, you two!"

Water was splashing, and mud was flying, and oaths were being sworn, and blows were being struck, when some more men went down into the ditch to help the sergeant, and dragged out my convict and the other one. Both were bleeding and panting and struggling.

"Mind!" said my convict, wiping blood from his face with his ragged sleeves. "*I* give him up to you!"

Said the sergeant; "It'll do you small good, my man, being in the same **plight** yourself. Handcuffs there!"

"I don't expect it to do me any good," said my convict, "I took him. He knows it. That's enough for me."

The other convict was **livid** and, in addition to the old bruised left side of his face, seemed to be torn all over. They were both handcuffed. The bruised convict leaned upon the guard to keep himself from falling.

DISDAINFULLY (diss <u>dane</u> fuh lee) *adv.*
as if someone or something is not worthy
Synonyms: scornfully, contemptuously

TORCH (torch) *n.*
a long stick that is set on fire
Synonyms: light, flame

ASSURE (uh <u>shur</u>) *v.* **-ing**, **-ed**
to make certain of
Synonyms: promise, ensure

INNOCENCE (<u>in</u> uh sense) *n.*
a state of not being guilty or not having
done harm
Synonyms: guiltlessness, blamelessness,
virtuousness

ATTENTIVE (uh <u>ten</u> tiv) *adj.*
giving careful thought to something
Synonyms: alert, focused, absorbed,
engrossed

"Take notice, guard, he tried to murder me," were his first words.

"Tried to murder him?" said my convict, **disdainfully**. "I took him, and giv' him up. I dragged him here!"

The other one still gasped, "He tried – he tried – to – murder me. Bear – bear witness."

"Lookee here!" said my convict to the sergeant. "Single-handed I got clear of the prisonship I made a dash. I could have got clear of these death-cold grounds if I had wanted – look at my leg. You won't find much iron on it! If I hadn't known that he was here, things would be different. Let him go free? Let him make a fool of me again? No, no, no."

"Enough of this talk," said the sergeant. "Light those **torches**."

My convict looked round him for the first time and saw me. I had been waiting for him to see me that I might try to **assure** him of my **innocence**. He gave me a look that I did not understand, his face **attentive**.

The soldier lighted three or four torches. "All right," said the sergeant. "March."

ENTRY (<u>en</u> tree) *n.*
   notation put into a book or record
      Synonym: note, record

REMARK (ri <u>mark</u>) *v.* **-ing**, **-ed**
   to take notice of in speech
      Synonyms: comment, declare

STARVE (starv) *v.* **-ing**, **-ed**
   to suffer from a lack of food
      Synonym: famish

We had not gone far when three cannon were fired ahead of us with a sound that seemed to burst something inside my ear. "You are expected on board," said the sergeant to my convict, "they know you are coming."

After an hour or so of this travelling, we came to a rough wooden hut. The sergeant there made some kind of report and some **entry** in a book. Then the other convict was taken off to go on board first.

My convict never looked at me except that once. Suddenly, he turned to the sergeant, and **remarked**, "I wish to say something about this escape. It may prevent some persons getting into trouble because of me."

"Say what you like," said the sergeant.

"A man can't **starve**, at least I can't. I took some wittles, up at the village over yonder."

"You mean stole," said the sergeant.

"From the blacksmith's."

"Halloa!" said the sergeant, staring at Joe.

"Halloa, Pip!" said Joe, staring at me.

"It was a pie."

FLING (fling) *v.* **-ing, flung**
    to throw hard
        Synonyms: heave, toss

HISSING (<u>hiss</u> ing) *adj.*
    to make an "sss" noise like a snake
        Synonym: whispering

"Have you happened to miss a pie, black-smith?" asked the sergeant.

"My wife did!"

"So," said my convict, turning his eyes on Joe, "I've eat your pie."

"God knows you're welcome to it," returned Joe. "We don't know what you have done, but we wouldn't have you starved to death for it, poor miserable fellow-creature. Would us, Pip?"

Then something clicked in the man's throat again, and he turned his back.

The boat had returned, and so we followed him and the guard to the landing and saw him put into the boat, which was rowed by a crew of convicts. By the light of the torches, we saw him taken up the side and disappear. Then, the torches were **flung hissing** into the water, and went out, as if it were all over with him.

As we made our way home, Joe and I, it was much upon my mind that I ought to tell Joe the whole truth. Yet I did not. The fear of losing Joe's trust tied up my tongue.

OFFENSE (uh <u>fenss</u>) *n.*
something that displeases, something that
breaks a custom or law
Synonyms: crime, scandal

ASSIST (uh <u>sisst</u>) *v.* **-ing**, **-ed**
to be of help
Synonym: aid

And then, as soon as I was home, my sister clutched at me as if I were an **offense** and then **assisted** me up to bed. Any secrets I had, I kept to myself.

APPRENTICE (uh <u>pren</u> tiss) *v.* **-ing**, **-ed**
    to arrange to learn a skill or trade from a
    skilled worker or tradesperson
        Synonym: train

FAVOR (<u>fay</u> vurred) *v.* **-ing**, **-ed**
    to be handled with special treatment
        Synonym: given

EMPLOYMENT (em <u>ploy</u> ment) *n.*
    a job or task
        Synonym: work

CHAPTER 3

When I was old enough, I was to be **apprenticed** to Joe, and until then, I was **favored** with any **employment** I could get.

I also did my best to keep learning. And I took all help I could get for that.

Mr. Wopsle's great-aunt kept an evening school in the village and a little shop. Biddy took care of the shop and sometimes I helped. Biddy was Mr. Wopsle's great-aunt's granddaughter, an

IMMENSELY (i <u>menss</u> lee) *adv.*
to a big extent, very
Synonyms: hugely, enormously

GRIM (grim) *adj.*
forbidding or gloomy in appearance
Synonyms: humorless, dour

POUNCE (pounss) *v.* **-ing, -ed**
to jump on something or someone suddenly
Synonym: leapt

KNEAD (<u>need</u>) *v.* **-ing, -ed**
to work or press into a mass (like bread dough)
Synonyms: stretch, manipulate

orphan like myself. Her hair always needed brushing, her hands always needed washing, and her shoes always needed soles. With Biddy's help, I struggled through the alphabet and bettered myself by learning to read.

One day, Mrs. Joe came home with Uncle Pumblechook from shopping, and they were both greatly excited.

"Miss Havisham who lives uptown, your uncle Pumblechook's landlady, wants this boy to go and play there!" she said to Joe. "And of course he's going. And he had better play there," said my sister, "or I'll work him."

I had heard of Miss Havisham uptown, an **immensely** rich and **grim** lady who lived in a large and unfriendly house and who led a lonely life.

"This boy's fortune may be made by his going to Miss Havisham's," said Mrs. Joe. "And Mr. Pumblecock has offered to take him tonight to his place and then to Miss Havisham's tomorrow morning!"

With that, she **pounced** upon me, and I was soaped and **kneaded** and put into clean linen

TWINKLE (<u>twing</u> kuhl) *v.* **-ing**, **-ed**
   to shine with a sparkling light
     Synonym: flicker

and my suit. I was then delivered over to Mr. Pumblechook.

"Good-bye, Joe!" I cried.

"God bless you, Pip, old chap!"

I had never parted from him before. I could at first see no stars. But they **twinkled** out one by one, without throwing any light on the questions why on earth I was going to play at Miss Havisham's and what on earth I was expected to play at.

As planned, I spent the night with the Pumblechook's, and by ten the next morning I was in front of Miss Havisham's house, which was of old brick and had a great many iron bars to it. A young lady came across the courtyard.

"This," said Mr. Pumblechook, "is Pip."

"This is Pip, is it?" returned the young lady, who was very pretty and seemed very proud; "Come in, Pip."

Mr. Pumblechook was coming in also, when she stopped him with the gate.

"Oh!" she said. "Not you!"

Mr. Pumblechook left with the words: "Boy!

BEHAVIOR (bee <u>have</u> yor) *n.*
how a person acts or conducts themselves
Synonyms: actions, deeds

CREDIT (<u>kred</u> it) *n.*
something that adds to a person's reputation
Synonyms: recognition, acknowledgment

SCORNFUL (<u>skorn</u> fuhl) *adj.*
having an attitude of looking down on
someone or something
Synonym: contemptuous

PASSAGE (<u>pass</u> ij) *n.*
a long hallway
Synonym: corridor

RIDICULOUS (rid <u>dik</u> yuh luhss) *adj.*
foolish looking or acting
Synonyms: silly, absurd, preposterous

Let your **behavior** here be a **credit** unto them which brought you up by hand!"

She locked the gate, and we went across the courtyard. She was about the same age as I, beautiful, and she was as **scornful** of me as if she had been twenty-one and a queen.

We went into the house by a side door. The **passages** were all dark. She took up a candle burning there, and we went through more passages and up a staircase.

At last we came to the door of a room. There she turned to me and said, "Go in."

I answered, more in shyness than politeness, "After you, miss."

To this she returned: "Don't be **ridiculous**, boy. I am not going in." And then she scornfully walked away from me, and took the candle with her.

I knocked and entered and found myself in a pretty large room, well lighted with wax candles. In an armchair sat the strangest lady I have ever seen or shall ever see.

She was dressed all in white satins and lace

VEIL (vale) *n.*
a lacy covering for the head or face
Synonym: covering

AVOID (uh <u>void</u>) *v.* **-ing, -ed**
1. to turn away from something, to dodge
Synonyms: sidestep, elude
2. to try to prevent something from happening
Synonyms: avert, fend off

UTTER (uh <u>ter</u>) *v.* **-ing, -ed**
to express something in words
Synonyms: say, state

DIVERSION (duh <u>vur</u> zhuhn) *n.*
something that takes your mind off other
things
Synonyms: change, digression, variation

and silks. And she had a long white **veil** hanging from her hair, which had bridal flowers in it. Some bright jewels sparkled on her neck and on her hands and on the table. Dresses and half-packed trunks were scattered about. She had not quite finished dressing, for she had but one shoe on.

"Who is it?" said the lady at the table.

"Pip, ma'am. Come – to play."

"Come nearer. Let me look at you."

It was when I stood before her, **avoiding** her eyes, that I saw that a clock in the room had stopped at twenty minutes to nine.

"Look at me," said Miss Havisham. "Do you know what I touch here?" she said, laying her hands on her left side.

"Your heart."

"Broken!" She **uttered** the word with an eager look that had a kind of boast in it.

"I am tired," said Miss Havisham. "I want **diversion**. Play. Call Estella. At the door."

To stand in the dark in a mysterious passage of an unknown house, calling Estella to a scornful young lady was almost as bad as playing to

BECKON (<u>bek</u> kon) *v.* **-ing, -ed**
to wave or motion to someone, to ask someone
to come to you
Synonyms: gesture, signal, summon

WITHERED (<u>with</u> urred) *adj.*
reduced in size, shrunken, or dried out
Synonyms: shriveled, wrinkled

SHROUD (shroud) *n.*
fabric used to cover a dead person
Synonym: burial cloth

order. But she answered at last, and her light came along the dark passage.

Miss Havisham **beckoned** her. "Let me see you play cards with this boy."

"With him? He's a common laboring boy!"

"Well? You can break his heart."

"What do you play, boy?" asked Estella, with the greatest disdain.

"Nothing but <u>beggar my neighbor</u>, miss."

So we sat down to cards.

It was then I began to understand that everything in the room had stopped, like the watch and the clock, a long time ago. I noticed that Miss Havisham put down the jewel exactly on the spot from which she had taken it up. The shoe on her table, once white, now yellow, had never been worn. I glanced down at the foot which did not have a shoe, and saw that the silk stocking on it, once white, now yellow, had been worn ragged. The **withered** bridal dress on Miss Havisham's form looked like <u>grave-clothes</u>. Her long veil looked like a **shroud**.

"He calls the <u>knaves</u> Jacks, this boy!" said

CONTEMPT (kuhn <u>tempt</u>) *n.*
a lack of respect
Synonyms: disdain, scorn

DENOUNCE (di <u>nounss</u>) *v.* **-ing**, **-ed**
to say in public that someone has done
something wrong or bad
Synonyms: accuse, condemn, blame

INSULTING (in <u>sult</u> ing) *adj.*
making fun or finding fault with someone or
something
Synonyms: mocking, disparaging

OPPORTUNITY (opp ur <u>too</u> nuh tee) *n.*
an occasion to do something
Synonym: chance

Estella with a superior air. "And what rough hands he has! And what thick boots!"

I had never thought of being ashamed of my hands before, but I began to think them a very common pair. Her **contempt** for me was so strong that it became catching.

She won the game and she **denounced** me for a stupid, clumsy laboring-boy.

Remarked Miss Havisham to me. "She says many hard things of you, but you say nothing of her. What do you think of her?"

"I think she is very proud," I replied, in a whisper.

"Anything else?"

"I think she is very pretty and very **insulting** and I think I should like to go home."

"And never see her again, though she is so pretty? Come again after six days!"

I followed the candle down. "Wait here, you boy," said Estella, and she disappeared.

I took the **opportunity** to look at my coarse hands and my common boots. They had never troubled me before, but they troubled me now.

VULGAR (<u>vuhl</u> gur) *adj.*
  in bad taste, low class
    Synonyms: rude, crude

GENTEELY (jen <u>teel</u> lee) *adv.*
  in a cultured way, with polish and refinement
    Synonyms: elegantly, sophisticatedly

INSOLENTLY (<u>in</u> suh luhnt lee) *adv.*
  in a disrespectful or insulting way
    Synonym: rudely

PONDER (<u>pon</u> dur) *v.* **-ing**, **-ed**
  to think about carefully
    Synonyms: consider, philosophize, muse

IGNORANT (<u>ig</u> nur uhnt) *adj.*
  without schooling, without knowledge
    Synonym: uneducated

They looked **vulgar**. I determined to ask Joe why he had ever taught me to call those picture-cards Jacks, which ought to be called knaves. I wished Joe had been rather more **genteely** brought up, and then I should have been so, too.

She came back with some bread and meat and a mug of drink. She put the mug down on the stones of the yard and gave me the bread and meat without looking at me, as **insolently** as if I were a dog in disgrace. Tears started in my eyes. The moment they sprang there, the girl looked at me with a delight in having been the cause of them.

After I had eaten, she pushed me out, and locked the gate. I set off on the four-mile walk to our forge, **pondering** on all I had seen. This girl had made me see that I was a common boy, that my hands were rough and my boots were thick. I had a disgusting habit of calling knaves Jacks and I was much more **ignorant** than I had thought myself last night.

When I reached home, my sister was very curious to know all about Miss Havisham's. She had no doubt that Miss Havisham would "do

PREMIUM (<u>pree</u> mee uhm) *n.*
an extra amount, a high price
Synonym: bonus

BINDING (bind) *v.* **-ing**, **bound**
to oblige, to have someone agree to do
something
Synonyms: hire, contract

something" for me. My sister held out for property or a handsome **premium** for **binding** me as an apprentice to some genteel trade.

And then, after my sister had gone to the kitchen, I told Joe in confidence that I felt very miserable, that there had been a beautiful young lady at Miss Havisham's who had said I was common, and that I wished I was not common.

I thought long after I went to bed how common Estella would think Joe, a mere blacksmith. I thought how Joe and my sister were sitting in the kitchen and how Miss Havisham and Estella never sat in a kitchen but were far above such common doings.

OCCUR (uh <u>kur</u>) *v.* **-ing, -ed**
   1. to take place
      Synonym: happen
   2. to come to mind
      Synonym: present itself

OBLIGED (ob <u>blijd</u>) *adj.*
   feeling indebted or obligated
      Synonyms: grateful, thankful

CHAPTER 4

The idea **occurred** to me a morning or two later that the best step I could take towards making myself uncommon was to get out of Biddy everything she knew. I said to Biddy when I went to visit that I had a reason for wishing to get on in life and that I should feel very much **obliged** to her if she would share all her learning with me. Biddy said she would, and indeed she began to carry out her promise within five

INSTRUMENT (<u>in</u> struh muhnt) *n.*
an object used for work
Synonym: tool

SPELLBOUND (spel <u>bound</u>) *adj.*
held as if by magic
Synonyms: fascinated, entranced

RECLINE (ree <u>kline</u>) *v.* **-ing, -ed**
to lean or lie back
Synonyms: rest, sprawl

minutes, sending me home with a copy of a large old English D, which she had copied from the headline of some newspaper.

When I left Biddy that evening, I went to a tavern in the village called the Three Jolly Bargemen, to call for Joe, who liked to smoke his pipe there. Joe greeted me as usual with "Halloa, Pip, old chap!" and the moment he said that I noticed a stranger beside him. The stranger turned his head and looked at me.

I had never seen this strange man before, but he seemed to know me. He stirred his rum and water pointedly at me – with my convict's file!

He did this so that nobody but I saw the file. Then he wiped the file and put it in a pocket. I knew that he knew my convict, the moment I saw the **instrument**. I was **spellbound**. But he **reclined**, taking little notice of me.

Joe got up to go, and took me by the hand.

"Stop, Mr. Gargery," said the strange man. "I've got a bright new coin in my pocket, and the boy shall have it."

CRUMPLED (<u>kruhm</u> puhld) *adj.*
  collapsed, made into many wrinkles and folds
    Synonym: crinkled

RESTORE (ri <u>stor</u>) *v.* **-ing**, **-ed**
  to give something back
    Synonym: return

ORNAMENTAL (or nuh <u>ment</u> al) *adj.*
  serving a visual rather than useful purpose
    Synonyms: decorative, attractive

COAX (kohks) *v.* **-ing**, **-ed**
  to gently persuade someone to do something
    Synonyms: cajole, convince

APPOINTED (uh <u>poin</u> td) *adj.*
  officially arranged or established
    Synonyms: planned, set, scheduled

He took out a handful of small change, then he folded it in some **crumpled** paper and gave it to me. "Yours!" said he.

I thanked him, and holding tight to Joe, we left.

Once at home, I took the money out of the paper. "But what's this?" said Mrs. Joe, throwing down the coin and catching up the paper. "Two one-pound notes folded over it!"

Joe ran with them to the tavern to **restore** them to their owner. Presently Joe came back, saying that the man was gone, but that he, Joe, had left word about the notes. Then my sister sealed the notes up in a piece of paper and put them under an **ornamental** teapot. There they remained, a nightmare to me.

That night I couldn't sleep. I kept thinking of the strange man and the convict file. I **coaxed** myself to sleep by thinking of Miss Havisham's, next Wednesday. And in my sleep I saw the file coming at me out of a door, without seeing who held it, and I screamed myself awake.

At the **appointed** time I returned to Miss

EPISODE (<u>ep</u> uh sode) *n.*
an event or set of events in a life or story
Synonyms: installment, incident

OPPRESSIVE (uh <u>press</u> iv) *adj.*
making you feel weighted down
Synonyms: heavy, smothering, burdensome

Havsham's, and my ring at the gate brought out Estella.

"Well? Am I pretty?" she asked.

"Yes, I think you are very pretty."

"Am I insulting?"

"Not so much as you were last time," said I.

She slapped my face. "Now?" said she. "You little monster, what do you think of me now?"

"I shall not tell you."

"Why don't you cry again?"

"Because I'll never cry for you again," said I. We went upstairs after this **episode**. We were soon in Miss Havisham's room, where she and everything else were just as I had left them. "Are you ready to play?" she said.

"I don't think I am, ma'am."

"Then are you willing to work?"

I nodded.

"Then go there," said she, pointing at the door, "and wait there until I come."

I entered the room. From that room, too, the daylight was completely gone, and it had an airless smell that was **oppressive**. Everything

PREPARATION (prep uh <u>ray</u> shun) *n.*
the process of being made ready
Synonym: anticipation

RUIN (<u>roo</u> in) *n.*
the destruction of something
Synonyms: decay, damage

was covered with dust and dropping to pieces. The biggest object was a long table with a tablecloth spread on it, as if a feast had been in **preparation** when the house and the clocks all stopped. "This," said Miss Havisham, pointing to the table with her cane, "is where I will be laid when I am dead." She pointed at the cobwebs. "That is a wedding cake. Mine!"

She then leaned on me and said, "Come, come, come! Walk me, walk me!"

I made out from this that the work I had to do was to walk Miss Havisham round and round the room. I started at once.

At last she stopped and said, "This is my birthday, Pip. When the **ruin** is complete," she said, "and when they lay me dead, in my bride's dress on the bride's table, so much the better if it is done on my birthday!"

She stood looking at the table as if she stood looking at her own figure lying there. I remained quiet until Estella returned.

In an instant, Miss Havisham said, "Let me see you two play cards." With that we returned

FORMER (<u>form</u> er) *adj.*
coming before or earlier
Synonyms: previous, preceding, prior

ENLARGE (en <u>larj</u>) *v.* **-ing, -ed**
to make more of
Synonyms: increase, amplify, expand

OCCUPATION (ok yuh <u>pay</u> shun) *n.*
what a person does for a living
Synonyms: job, profession, business

TOLERATE (<u>tol</u> uh rate) *v.* **-ing, -ed**
to put up with or endure
Synonyms: accept, bear

to her room and sat down and played while Miss Havisham watched.

When we had played some half-dozen games, a day was named for my return, and I was taken down into the yard to be fed in the **former** dog-like manner.

"You may kiss me, if you like," Estella said.

I kissed her cheek. I felt that the kiss was given to the common boy and that it was worth nothing and I went home.

After that day, I began to visit Miss Havisham more and more. And as we began to be more used to each other, Miss Havisham talked more to me and asked me such questions as what had I learned and what I was going to be. I told her I was going to be apprenticed to Joe, I believed, and I **enlarged** upon my knowing nothing else and waited hopefully for her to offer me some different **occupation**. But she did not. Neither did she ever give me any money.

Estella was always around. Sometimes, she would coldly **tolerate** me, sometimes she would tell me that she hated me. Miss Havisham would

INFLUENCE (<u>in</u> floo enss) *v.* **-ing, -ed**
  to change or have an effect on someone or
  something
    Synonyms: alter, sway

COUNCIL (<u>koun</u> suhl) *n.*
  a discussion by a group of people
    Synonyms: meeting, conference

PROSPECT (<u>pross</u> pekt) *n.*
  something expected or looked forward to
    Synonym: hope

OVERWHELMED (oh vur <u>whelmd</u>) *adj.*
  strongly affected
    Synonyms: overcome, carried away

SIGNIFY (<u>sig</u> nif eye) *v.* **-ing, -ed**
  to make something known
    Synonyms: point out, signal

often ask me in a whisper, "Does she grow prettier and prettier, Pip?" Sometimes she would murmur to Estella, "Break their hearts my pride and hope!"

What could I become with these surroundings? How could my character fail to be **influenced** by them?

I kept complete confidence in no one but Biddy. Why it came natural to me to do so, and why Biddy had a deep concern in everything I told her, I did not know then.

Meanwhile, **councils** went on in the kitchen at home, talking about my **prospects**. I was old enough to be apprenticed to Joe, and he was not happy about my being taken from the forge, even if that be Miss Havisham's wish.

But to my dismay, it was not her wish.

"You had better be apprenticed at once," she told me one day. "Would the blacksmith come here with you, and bring the necessary papers?"

I was **overwhelmed**, but I **signified** that I had no doubt he would take it as an honor to be asked.

"Then let him come soon."

When I got home at night and delivered this

TRIAL (<u>trye</u> uhl) *n.*
    a difficult experience, something that tests one
        Synonym: ordeal

ARRAY (uh <u>ray</u>) *v.* **-ing, -ed**
    to dress in finery
        Synonym: arranging

ACCOMPANY (uh <u>kom</u> puh nee) *v.* **-ing, -ed**
    to go along with someone
        Synonyms: join, escort

INTENTION (in <u>ten</u> shuhn) *n.*
    something that you mean to do
        Synonyms: plan, design, purpose

MISCHIEVOUSLY (<u>miss</u> chuh vuhss lee) *adv.*
    with teasing behavior
        Synonyms: playfully, annoyingly

message for Joe, my sister burst into sobbing. My expectations did not seem so great to her just then.

It was a **trial** to my feelings, on the next day, to see Joe **arraying** himself in his Sunday clothes to **accompany** me to Miss Havisham's. It was not for me to tell him that he looked far better in his working-dress. I knew he made himself uncomfortable for me.

Joe and I held straight on to Miss Havisham's house. Estella opened the gate as usual, and took us to Miss Havisham, who was seated at her table.

"Well!" said Miss Havisham. "And you have raised the boy, with the **intention** of taking him for your apprentice? Does the boy like the trade?"

"I believe he likes it," said Joe.

"Have you brought the papers with you?" asked Miss Havisham.

He gave them, not to Miss Havisham, but to me. I know I was ashamed of him when I saw that Estella's eyes laughed **mischievously**. I took the papers out of his hand and gave them to Miss Havisham.

CONVICTION (kuhn <u>vik</u> shuhn) *n.*
a deep belief in something
Synonyms: assurance, certainty

MAGNIFICENT (mag <u>nif</u> i sent) *adj.*
impressive
Synonyms: imposing, monumental,
splendid

"Pip has earned money here," she said, "and here it is, in this bag. Give it to your master, Pip and then Estella shall let you out."

"Am I to come again?" I asked.

"No. Gargery is your master now"

In another minute we were outside the gate, and Estella was gone. Joe backed up against a wall and said to me, "Astonishing!"

I was bound then as an apprentice to Joe. When I got into my little bedroom that night, I was truly wretched, and I had a strong **conviction** that I should never like Joe's trade. I had liked it once, but once was not now.

It is a most miserable thing to feel ashamed of home. Home had never been a very pleasant place to me, because of my sister's temper. But Joe had made it good for me. I had believed in our living room as being most elegant. I had believed in the kitchen as **magnificent**. I had believed in the forge as the glowing road to manhood and independence. Within a single year all this was changed. Now it was all coarse and common.

EDUCATION (edj yoo <u>kay</u> shun) *n.*
the process of gaining or giving knowledge
Synonyms: instruction, schooling,
tutelage

ACQUIRE (uh <u>kwire</u>) *v.* **-ing**, **-ed**
to get something
Synonyms: obtain, attain, gain

REPROACH (ri prohch) *n.*
disapproval
Synonyms: blame, disgrace, contempt

What I dreaded was that I should lift up my eyes and see Estella looking in at one of the windows of the forge. I was afraid that she would find me with a black face and hands, doing the coarsest part of my work, and that she would despise me.

Whatever **education** I **acquired** from Biddy I tried to give to Joe. I wanted to make Joe less ignorant and common, so he might be worthier of me and less open to Estella's **reproach**.

In between trying to educate Joe, I found myself again going to Miss Havisham's.

Everything was unchanged, and Miss Havisham was alone.

"Well?" said she, fixing her eyes upon me. "I hope you want nothing? You'll get nothing."

"No, indeed, Miss Havisham. I only wanted you to know that I am doing very well in my apprenticeship, and I am always thankful to you."

"There, there!" she said. "You are looking round for Estella? She's in Europe," said Miss Havisham, "Becoming educated, admired by all. Do you feel that you have lost her?"

DISSASTISFIED (dis <u>sat</u> uhss fide) *adj.*
not content
Synonyms: discontent, displeased

ROUTINE (roo <u>teen</u>) *n.*
a regular way of doing something
Synonyms: pattern, method, procedure

There was such a terrible enjoyment in her words that I was at a loss what to say. She saved me the trouble by sending me away. When the gate was closed upon me, I felt more than ever **dissatisfied** with my home and with my trade and with everything.

I now fell into a **routine** of apprenticeship life. I continued at heart to hate my trade and to be ashamed of home. The only thing to do was to try to better myself.

"Biddy," said I, "I want to be a gentleman."

"Oh, I wouldn't, if I was you!" she returned, "Don't you think you are happier as you are?"

"Biddy," I exclaimed, impatiently, "I am not at all happy as I am. If I could have been but half as fond of the forge as I was when I was little, I know it would have been much better for me. You and I and Joe would have wanted nothing then, and Joe and I would perhaps have become partners when I was out of my time. How would I know I was coarse and common, if nobody had told me so!"

"It was neither a very true nor a very polite

SOOTHING (<u>soo</u> thing) *adj.*
  comforting
    Synonyms: calming, quieting

RELISH (<u>rel</u> ish) *v.* **-ing**, **-ed**
  to like something a great deal
    Synonyms: enjoy, appreciate, treasure

DERIVE (di <u>rive</u>) *v.* **-ing**, **-ed**
  to take or receive from a source
    Synonyms: obtain, earn

HONEST (<u>on</u> est) *adj.*
  being truthful and good
    Synonyms: moral, principled

thing to say," she remarked. "Who said such a thing?"

I answered, "The beautiful young lady at Miss Havisham's, and I want to be a gentleman on her account."

Biddy patted my shoulder in a **soothing** way.

With Biddy being so kind and warm, I thought it would be very good for me if I could get Estella out of my head. Then I could go to work determined to **relish** what I had to do. I knew if Estella were beside me instead of Biddy she would make me miserable. We talked a good deal as we walked, and all that Biddy said seemed right. Biddy was never insulting. She would have **derived** only pain from giving me pain. How could it be, then, that I did not like her much the better of the two?

"Biddy," said I, "If I could only get myself to fall in love with you!"

"But you never will," said Biddy.

I kept thinking that Biddy was better than Estella and that the plain **honest** working life to which I was born had nothing in it to be ashamed

SUFFICIENT (suh <u>fish</u> uhnt) *adj.*
enough in quantity
Synonyms: ample, adequate

of but offered me **sufficient** means of self-respect and happiness. And then, just as I felt better, I would think that perhaps Miss Havisham was going to make my fortune when my time was out, after all, and all my thoughts would scatter like leaves.

APPROACH (uh <u>prohch</u>) *v.* **-ing**, **-ed**
to move nearer
Synonyms: close in, near

PRIVATE (<u>prye</u> vit) *adj.*
not meant to be known or shared
Synonyms: confidential, secret

CONFERENCE (<u>kon</u> fur uhnss) *n.*
a formal discussion
Synonyms: meeting, council

CHAPTER 5

It was in the fourth year of my apprenticeship to Joe. We were at the Three Jolly Bargemen one Saturday night, when a strange gentleman **approached** us. "You are the blacksmith?" he asked, and Joe nodded.

Then he turned to me. "You are Pip?" he asked. When I nodded he said he wanted to have a **private conference** with me and with Joe, at our home, which we went to right away.

"My name," he said, when we were all

CONFIDENTIAL (<u>kon</u> fuh den shuhl) *adj.*
  trusted with private matters
    Synonyms: secret, personal

AGENT (<u>ay</u> juhnt) *n.*
  someone who acts or does business for another
    Synonyms: representative, envoy, deputy

CANCEL (<u>kan</u> suhl) *v.* **-ing**, **-ed**
  to put an end to something, to make something
  no longer in effect
    Synonyms: call off, nullify, end

REQUEST (ri <u>kwest</u>) *n.*
  the act of asking for something
    Synonyms: appeal, demand

seated, "is Jaggers, and I am a lawyer in London. I have unusual business with you. I am the **confidential agent** of another."

"Now, Joseph Gargery, I am the bearer of an offer to remove from you your apprentice. You would not object to **cancel** his apprenticeship for his good? You would want nothing for doing this?"

"Lord forbid that I should want anythink for not standing in Pip's way," said Joe, staring.

"Very well," said Mr. Jaggers. "What I have to say is that he has Great Expectations."

Joe and I gasped and looked at one another.

"I am to tell him," said Mr. Jaggers, "that he will come into a handsome property. Further, he must be immediately removed from this place, and be brought up as a gentleman. In a word, he is a young man of great expectations."

I held my breath. Miss Havisham was going to make my fortune on a grand scale!

"Now, Mr. Pip," pursued the lawyer, "You are to understand, first, that it is the **request** of the person who gave me my orders that you always

REVEAL (ri <u>veel</u>) *v.* **-ing**, **-ed**
to make known something that was previously
hidden or secret
Synonyms: disclose, divulge, unveil

PROHIBITED (proh <u>hib</u> it ed) *adj.*
not allowed
Synonyms: banned, forbidden, barred

STAMMER (<u>stam</u> ur) *v.* **-ing**, **-ed**
to repeat sounds, to speak in an unsure way
Synonym: stutter

MAINTENANCE (<u>mayn</u> tuh nenss) *n.*
the act of keeping something in working order
Synonyms: upkeep, preservation

GUARDIAN (<u>gar</u> dee uhn) *n.*
someone who watches over or has
responsibility for something or someone
Synonyms: protector, custodian

bear the name of Pip. Now you are to understand, secondly, that the name of the person who is giving you this remains a secret until the person chooses to **reveal** it. It may be years away. Now, you are **prohibited** from asking any questions on this. Your acceptance of these conditions is binding. I am not responsible for the person who gave me these conditions. That person gives you your expectations, not me. The secret of who that person is is only held by that person and by me. If you have any objection, this is the time to speak out."

I **stammered** that I had no objection.

"I should think not! Now, Mr. Pip, we come next to the details of the arrangement. There is a sum of money that is more than enough for your education and **maintenance**. You will please consider me your **guardian**."

"First," said Mr. Jaggers, "you should have some new clothes. You'll want some money. I think the sooner you leave here, as you are to be a gentleman, the better. You shall receive my printed address. You can take a coach to London and come straight to me."

CONGRATULATE (kuhn <u>grach</u> uh late) *v.* **-ing**, **-ed**
to express praise for a person's achievement
Synonyms: applaud, cheer

RESENT (ri <u>zent</u>) *v.* **-ing**, **-ed**
to feel annoyance or ill will
Synonym: dislike

FURNISHED (<u>fur</u> nishd) *adj.*
filled with furniture and household basics
Synonyms: equipped, outfitted,
supplied

I thanked him and he left. Joe was seated by the kitchen fire, gazing at the burning coals. I too sat down before the fire and nothing was said for a long time.

Later, we went to tell my sister and Biddy. Mrs. Joe was ill, and Biddy was helping to care for her. After a pause, they both **congratulated** me, but there was a certain touch of sadness in their congratulations that I rather **resented**.

I took it upon myself to make sure everyone knew nothing and said nothing about the maker of my fortune. Nothing was to be said, except that I had come into great expectations from a mysterious person. They talked about my going away and about what they should do without me.

That night, when I got into my little room, I took a long look at it. I was going to much better rooms, but this room was **furnished** with memories. I felt suddenly upset, the same way as when I thought of the difference between Biddy and Estella or the forge and Miss Havisham's. I closed my eyes and tried to sleep.

CONSIDERABLE (kuhn <u>sid</u> uh ruh buhl) *adj.*
   large in size or degree
      Synonyms: significant, substantial

SYMPATHETIC (sim puh <u>thet</u> ik) *adj.*
   able to share others' feeling
      Synonyms: compassionate, understanding

BESTOW (<u>bi stoh</u>) *v.* **-ing, -ed**
   to give someone something
      Synonyms: give, present, donate, confer

Morning made a **considerable** difference in brightening the way I felt. Joe and Biddy were very **sympathetic** and pleasant when I spoke of my leaving them, but they only spoke of it when I did. After breakfast Joe brought out my apprenticeship papers, and we put them in the fire, and I felt that I was free.

I bought new clothes, and then on Friday morning I went to pay my visit to Miss Havisham.

Miss Havisham was in the room with the long table, leaning on her crutch.

"I start for London, Miss Havisham, tomorrow," I was careful what I said, "and I thought you would kindly not mind my taking leave of you."

She made her cane play round me, as if she, the fairy godmother who had changed me, were **bestowing** the finishing gift.

"I have come into such good fortune since I saw you last, Miss Havisham," I said. "And I am so grateful for it, Miss Havisham!"

"I have seen Mr. Jaggers. I have heard about it, Pip. So you go tomorrow. And you have been

ADOPT (uh <u>dopt</u>) *v.* **-ing**, **-ed**
to be taken into a family or group
Synonyms: take up, foster

adopted by a rich person who is not named? And Mr. Jaggers is your guardian?"

"Yes, Miss Havisham."

"Well!" she went on, "You have a promising career before you. You follow Mr. Jaggers's instructions. Good-bye, Pip."

She stretched out her hand, and I left my fairy godmother standing in the midst of the dimly lighted room beside the rotten wedding cake that was hidden in cobwebs.

The village was very peaceful and quiet. I had been so little and without experience there, and all beyond was so unknown and great, that in a moment, with a sob, I broke into tears.

The journey from our town to the city was a journey of about five hours.

Mr. Jaggers' address, which he had sent me, was Little Britain. I presently arrived there, at a gloomy street. There I found an open door, painted with the name MR. JAGGERS.

My guardian let me into his own room, and told me what arrangements he had made for me. I was to go to Barnard's Inn, to young Mr. Herbert

TUTOR (<u>too</u> tur) *n.*

someone who gives private lessons

Synonyms: teacher, instructor, mentor

LIBERAL (<u>lib</u> ur uhl) *adj.*

marked by generosity

Synonyms: ample, abundant, plentiful

IMPOVERISHED (im <u>poh</u> ver rishd) *adj.*

having little or no money

Synonyms: poor, needy, destitute

MERCHANT (<u>mur</u> chuhnt) *n.*

someone who buys and sells goods

Synonyms: trader, shopkeeper

EXTRAVAGANT (ek <u>strav</u> uh guhnt) *adj.*

spending money too freely or foolishly

Synonyms: wasteful, squandering

DISINHERIT (diss in <u>hair</u> it) *v.* **-ing**, **-ed**

to prevent someone from obtaining property
after one's death

Synonym: cut off

HEIRESS (<u>air</u> ess) *n.*

a woman who is or who will be left money or
property

Synonyms: recipient, legatee

Pocket's rooms, the son of my **tutor**, Matthew Pocket, who was a relative of Miss Havisham's. I was told what my allowance was to be, and it was a very **liberal** one.

I took an immediate liking to Herbert Pocket. My fortune had been made for me. Herbert, however, was an **impoverished** gentleman, though he hoped to be a shipping **merchant** and he said he could help me to become more of a gentleman, as well. Best of all, he could tell me more about Miss Havisham.

"Her mother died when she was a baby, and her father was very rich and very proud. So was his daughter," said Herbert.

"Miss Havisham was an only child?" I asked.

"She had a half-brother. He turned out to be **extravagant** and altogether bad. At last his father **disinherited** him, but he softened when he was dying and left him well off, though not nearly so well off as Miss Havisham."

"Miss Havisham was now an **heiress**, and a great catch for a future husband. Her half-brother

AMPLE (<u>am</u> puhl) *adj.*
more than enough
Synonyms: abundant, plentiful

GRUDGE (<u>gruhj</u>) *n.*
a bad feeling towards someone
Synonyms: resentment, animosity

RECOVER (ri <u>kuhv</u> ur) *v.* **-ing**, **-ed**
to get better
Synonym: recuperate

CONSPIRACY (kuhn <u>spihr</u> uh see) *n.*
a plan made by two or more people that no one
else knows about
Synonyms: plot, intrigue

PROFIT (<u>prof</u> it) *n.*
a gain in money
Synonyms: proceeds, benefit

had now **ample** means again, but he wasted them once more. He held a **grudge** against her because he believed she was the father's favorite. One day, there appeared a man who pursued Miss Havisham. She loved him, and he got great sums of money from her.

The marriage day was fixed, the wedding dresses were bought, the wedding guests were invited. The day came, but not the bridegroom. He wrote her a letter."

"Which she received," I struck in, "when she was dressing for her marriage? At twenty minutes to nine?"

"At that hour and minute," said Herbert, nodding, "at which she afterwards stopped all the clocks. The letter broke off the marriage, but I can't tell you what else was in it. She became ill, and when she **recovered** she laid waste the whole place, and she has never since looked upon daylight. It has been said that the man she loved acted with her half-brother, that it was a **conspiracy** between them and that they shared the **profits**."

SCHEME (skeem) *n.*

a plan to do something, usually involving
deception

Synonyms: plot, strategy, ploy

ADVANCEMENT (ad <u>vanss</u> mint) *n.*

a move forward

Synonym: improvement

BENEFACTRESS (ben uh <u>fack</u> tress) *n.*

a woman who gives someone money or power
without expecting anything in return

Synonym: contributor

"I wonder why he didn't marry her and get all the property," said I.

"He may have been married already, or her shame may have been a part of her half-brother's **scheme**," said Herbert.

"What became of the two men?" I asked.

"They fell into deeper shame and ruin."

"Are they alive now?"

"I don't know." He paused and then told me that Estella was adopted by Miss Havisham, but he could not say when.

Then he told me that he would keep my secret. "I will not ask to whom you owe your **advancement**. It will never be asked by me or by anyone in my family."

In truth, he said this with so much care, that I felt the subject done with. Yet he said it with so much meaning, too, that I felt he as perfectly understood Miss Havisham to be my **benefactress**, as I understood the fact myself.

After two or three days I had set myself up in my room and had ordered all I wanted from different stores. Then Mr. Pocket, Herbert's father

PROFESSION (pruh fesh uhn) *n.*
way of making a living, occupation
Synonyms: career, employment, specialty

PROSPEROUS (<u>pross</u> per us) *adj.*
having a great deal of money
Synonyms: rich, wealthy, sucessful

CIRCUMSTANCE (<u>sur</u> kuhm stanss) *n.*
the situation in which someone lives or finds oneself
Synonyms: condition, position

and my tutor, and I had a long talk together. He knew that I was not designed for any **profession** and that I should be well enough educated if I could "hold my own" with the average young men in **prosperous circumstances**. He advised me to let him direct all my studies. He hoped that with his help I should meet with little to discourage me. I kept my bedroom in Barnard's Inn, and Herbert was my constant companion and friend.

I worked hard at my education. I soon had expensive habits, and I began to spend an amount of money that a few months before I should never have imagined. But through good and evil, I stuck to my books.

Occasionally, I dined with Mr. Jaggers. Dinner was laid in the best of the rooms, and we were served our food by his housekeeper.

She was a woman of about forty, with large faded eyes and streaming hair. Whenever she was in the room, she kept her eyes on my guardian, and it seemed she dreaded him. When she passed him, he clapped his large hand on hers, like a trap.

SCARRED (skarrd) *adj.*
   permanently marked
      Synonyms: cut, disfigured

SINEW (<u>sin</u> yoo) *n.*
   a band of tissue that connects muscle to bone
      Synonyms: tendon, fiber

"If you talk of strength," said Mr. Jaggers, "I'll show you a wrist. Molly, show your wrist."

"Master," she said, with her eyes fixed upon him. "Don't."

"Molly," said Mr. Jaggers, "Let us see!"

He took his hand from hers, and turned that wrist up on the table. It was deeply **scarred**.

Mr. Jaggers, coolly traced out the **sinews** with his finger. "Very few men have the power of wrist that this woman has." He nodded at her. "You can go now." She pulled back her hands and went out of the room. And I thought nothing of it. Not until much later would the meaning become clear to me.

CONFESS (kon <u>fess</u>) *v.* **-ing**, **-ed**
to be completely honest, to tell something that
was kept secret
Synonyms: admit, acknowledge

PLEASURE (<u>plezh</u> ur) *n.*
the state of being pleased
Synonyms: delight, enjoyment

CHAPTER 6

I was so busy, I hadn't time to think of home. But one day, to my great surprise, I received a letter. It read: "My Dear Mr. Pip: I write this for Mr. Gargery. He is going to London and would be glad if you might be willing to see him. Signed, BIDDY."

Let me **confess** my feelings. I was bound to Joe by so many ties, but I felt no **pleasure** and great shame. If I could have kept him away by

OBJECTION (ob <u>jek</u> shun) *n.*
a feeling or declaration of disapproval
Synonyms: disagreement, protest

SENSITIVENESS (<u>sen</u> suh tiv ness) *n.*
1. an awareness of other peoples' feelings
Synonyms: sympathy, comprehension
2. the state of being easily hurt
Synonym: delicacy

SPLENDID (<u>splen</u> did) *adj.*
noteworthy for luxury or beauty
Synonyms: magnificent, dazzling, grand

PETTISHLY (<u>pe</u> tish lee) *adv.*
in a mean or irritated way
Synonyms: crossly, disagreeably, grumpily

PERSONALLY (<u>pur</u> suh nuhl lee) *adv.*
without anyone else, in a personal manner
Synonyms: alone, individually

paying money, I would have. I had little **objection** to his being seen by Herbert or his father, both of whom I respected, but I had the sharpest **sensitiveness** of Joe's being seen by others I knew.

However, he was coming, that was certain. I came into town on Monday night to be ready for Joe, and I got up early in the morning, and made the living room **splendid**.

I heard Joe on the staircase.

With his good honest face all glowing and shining, he caught both my hands. "How are you, sir?" he asked.

"Joe," I interrupted, **pettishly**, "How can you call me, sir?"

"You're a gentlemen," he said. "And I have come **personally** to tell you news. Miss Havisham wishes to speak to you. Estella has come home and would be glad to see you.'"

I felt my face fire up.

"I asked Biddy to write the message to you," he said. "Biddy says, 'I know he will be very glad to have it by word of mouth. You want to see

REPENTANCE (ri <u>pent</u> tenss) *n.*
a feeling of being deeply sorry for something
you have done
Synonyms: guilt, contrition

INCONVENIENCE (in kuhn <u>veen</u> yuhnss) *n.*
trouble or difficulty
Synonyms: bother, annoyance, disruption

him, so go!' And seeing as I did want to see you, more than anythink in this world, I did go, and here I am!" he said. He rose from his chair.

"But you are not going now, Joe?"

"Yes, I am," said Joe.

"But you are coming back to dinner, Joe?"

"No, I am not," said Joe.

Our eyes met, and he gave me his hand.

"Pip, dear old chap, you and me is not to be together in London. I'm wrong in these clothes. I'm wrong out of the forge. You won't find half so much fault in me if you think of me in my forge dress." He touched me gently on the forehead and went out. As soon as I could recover myself, I hurried out after him and looked for him in the neighboring streets, but he was gone.

It was clear that I must go to our town next day, and in the first flow of my **repentance**, it was clear that I must stay at Joe's. But, when I had got my coach, I began to invent reasons and make excuses for putting up at the Blue Boar Hotel instead. I should be an **inconvenience** at Joe's.

CUSTOMARY (<u>kuhss</u> tuh mer ee) *adj.*
done most of the time
Synonyms: usual, regular

DISCHARGED (diss <u>charjd</u>) *adj.*
set free from prison or a task
Synonyms: let go, released

DIALOGUE (<u>dye</u> uh log) *n.*
speech between two or more people
Synonyms: conversation, conference

I was not expected. I should be too far from Miss Havisham's.

I was on the afternoon coach. At that time, it was **customary** to carry convicts down to the docks by coach. There were two convicts going down with me, handcuffed together, with irons on their legs. I looked at one of the convicts and knew his eyes at one glance. There stood the mysterious man from the Three Jolly Bargemen who had given me the shilling wrapped in the two one-pound notes!

I knew him, but he seemed not to know me. Still, I felt the convict's breathing, not only on the back of my head, but all along my spine.

"Two one-pound notes!" said one convict. "Where did he get them?"

"He had 'em hidden away," replied the other. "Then he asks me, 'You're going to be **discharged**?' Yes, I was I said. Then he asks would I find that boy that had fed him and kept his secret. And, once I had, could I give him them two one-pound notes? Yes, I would, I said. And I did."

After overhearing this **dialogue**, I would

SUSPICION (suh <u>spish</u> uhn) *n.*
> a thought or feeling that something is wrong
>> Synonyms: doubt, distrust, misgiving

IDENTITY (eye <u>den</u> ti tee) *n.*
> the characteristics by which someone or
> something is known
>> Synonym: individuality

COINCIDENCE (koh <u>in</u> si duhnss) *n.*
> 1. the state of occupying the same position
> or time
>> Synonym: coexistence
> 2. by accident, happening without plan
>> Synonyms: chance, accident, fluke

ARCHLY (<u>arch</u> lee) *adv.*
> in a playful way
>> Synonyms: mischievously, slyly

have jumped from the coach onto the highway, if I had not thought he had no **suspicion** of my **identity**. Indeed, I was so differently dressed that it was not at all likely he could have known. Still, the **coincidence** of our being together on the coach filled me with a dread that some other coincidence might at any moment connect me with my name. For this reason, I got off the coach as soon as we got to town. I walked to the hotel, trembling.

The next morning, early, I went to see Miss Havisham. She had adopted Estella, she had as good as adopted me, and it could not fail to be her intention to bring us together now.

She was in her chair near the old table, in the old dress. Sitting near her, was an elegant lady whom I had never seen.

"Come in, Pip," Miss Havisham said.

"I heard, Miss Havisham," said I, "that you wished to see me."

The strange lady looked **archly** at me, and then I saw that the eyes were Estella's eyes. But she was so much more beautiful. "Do you find

CONFUSEDLY (kuhn <u>fyooz</u> uhd lee) *adv.*
in an uncomprehending or disorganized way
Synonyms: aimlessly, frantically

DIASAGREEABLE (diss uh <u>gree</u> uh buhl) *adj.*
having a quarrelsome manner
Synonyms: bad-tempered, rude

PRESENCE (<u>prez</u> uhnss) *n.*
the state of being at a place or time
Synonyms: attendance, existence

GENTILITY (jen <u>til</u> uh tee) *n.*
a high or improved position in society, the
manners or behavior of those who have money
and power
Synonyms: sophisication, respectability,
polish

her much changed, Pip?" asked Miss Havisham with her greedy look.

"When I came in, I saw nothing of Estella, but now she almost looks like the old—"

"What? You are not going to say the old Estella?" Miss Havisham interrupted. "She was proud and insulting, and you wanted to go away from her. Don't you remember?"

I said **confusedly** that that was long ago. Estella smiled and said she had no doubt of my having been quite right, and of her having been very **disagreeable**.

"Is he changed?" Miss Havisham asked her.

"Very much," said Estella, looking at me.

"Less coarse and common?" said Miss Havisham.

Estella laughed. She treated me as a boy still.

She had just come home from France, and she was going to London. Her **presence** made me think of how I had wanted money and **gentility** and of how I had grown to be ashamed of my home and of Joe.

It was settled that I should stay there all the

HAUGHTY (<u>haw</u> tee) *adj.*
proud
Synonyms: arrogant, conceited

TONE (tohn) *n.*
a way of speaking that shows your feelings
Synonyms: inflection, intonation

OBSERVATION (ob zur <u>vay</u> shuhn) *n.*
the noting of a fact or occurrence
Synonyms: comment, remark

DEVOTION (di <u>vo</u> shun) *n.*
loving someone or something totally
Synonyms: commitment, allegiance

SUBMISSION (suhb <u>mi</u> shun) *n.*
the act of giving oneself up to another's power
Synonyms: compliance, capitulation

rest of the day and return to the hotel at night and to London tomorrow.

"Since your change of fortune, you have changed your companions," said Estella.

"Naturally," said I.

"And," she added, in a **haughty tone**, "what was fit company for you once would be quite unfit company for you now."

I doubt very much whether I had any intention left of going to see Joe, but if I had this **observation** put it to flight.

"Is she beautiful? Do you admire her?"

"Everybody must, Miss Havisham."

She drew my head close down to hers as she sat in the chair. "Love her, love her, love her! If she favors you, love her. If she tears your heart to pieces, love her! I adopted her to be loved. I raised her and educated her to be loved. I developed her to be loved. Love her!"

"I'll tell you," said she, in the same hurried whisper, "I know what real love is. It is blind **devotion**, it is unquestioning and utter **submission**, it is giving up your whole

COMPLY (kuhm <u>plye</u>) *v.* **-ing**, **-ed**
to act in agreement with another's command
Synonyms: agree, consent

GROPE (<u>grohp</u>) *v.* **-ing**, **-ed**
to feel one's way blindly
Synonyms: flounder, fumble

heart and soul to the one who hurts you – as I did!"

She rose up in the chair, in her shroud of a dress, and struck at the air. As I drew her down into her chair, to my surprise, I was suddenly aware of my guardian in the room.

Miss Havisham had seen him as soon as I, and was afraid of him.

"And so you are here, Pip?" he said.

I told him when I had arrived and how I had been asked me to come and see Estella.

"Go with Pip to dinner," ordered Miss Havisham.

He **complied**, and we **groped** our way down the dark stairs together. I waited for him to tell me that Miss Havisham was my benefactor but he did not. Later, after dinner, when I was back in my room at the Blue Boar, I heard Miss Havisham's words sounding in my ears: "Love her, love her, love her." Slowly, I adapted them, saying into my pillow, "I love her, I love her, I love her." But when would she begin to be interested in me? When would I awaken the

CONTEMPTUOUS (kuhn <u>tempt</u> you uhss) *adj.*
showing scorn
Synonyms: disdainful, disrespectful,
haughty

heart within her? And Joe? Forgotten, because I knew she would be **contemptuous** of him.

ACCUSTOMED (uh <u>kuss</u> tuhmd) *adj.*
 having a certain habit or custom
  Synonyms: habituated, used

UNEASINESS (uhn <u>ee</u> zee ness) *n.*
 a disturbed state
  Synonyms: unrest, disquiet, restlessness

LAVISH (<u>lav</u> ish) *adj.*
 spending freely, marked by excess
  Synonyms: extravagant, immoderate

CHAPTER 7

As I had grown **accustomed** to my expectations, I had begun to notice their effect. I lived in a state of **uneasiness** about my behavior toward Joe and Biddy. I should have been happier and better if I had never seen Miss Havisham's face and had been content to be partners with Joe in the honest old forge.

My **lavish** habits led Herbert's easy nature

EXPENSE (eks <u>penss</u>) *n.*
money spent in order to live
Synonyms: bill, cost, expenditure

ANXIETY (ang <u>zye</u> uh tee) *n.*
worry or fear
Synonyms: nervousness, concern, agitation

PROPOSAL (pruh <u>poz</u> uhl) *n.*
something put forward or suggested
Synonyms: plan, offer

HAUNT (hawnt) *v.* **-ing**, **-ed**
to come as a ghost, to visit often
Synonyms: frequent, appear, attend

into **expenses** that he could not afford and gave him many **anxieties**. I began to have a huge debt. Herbert soon followed.

I would willingly have taken Herbert's expenses on myself, but Herbert was proud, and I could make no such **proposal** to him. So he got into trouble in every direction. We spent as much money as we could.

And then, while money was being lost to me, so was family. Some days later I received news Mrs. J. Gargery had died on Monday last at twenty minutes past six in the evening, and I was to come to the funeral on Monday next at three o'clock in the afternoon.

It was the first time that a grave had opened in my road of life. The figure of my sister in her chair by the kitchen fire **haunted** me night and day.

Whatever my fortunes might have been, I could not have remembered my sister with much tenderness. But I had a shock of feeling. I went down early in the morning, and got to the Blue Boar and walked over to the forge.

MODEST (<u>mod</u> ist) *adj.*
1. following proper dress and behavior
   Synonym: demure
2. in a simple way
   Synonyms: humble, unassuming

REGRET (ri <u>gret</u>) *n.*
expression of distress, especially a feeling of
sadness about something done or not done
   Synonyms: sorrow, guilt

Poor dear Joe was seated apart at the upper end of the room; "Dear Joe, how are you?" He took my hand and said no more.

Biddy, looking very neat and **modest** in her black dress, went quietly here and there and was very helpful. When I had spoken to Biddy, I went and sat down near Joe.

We went into the churchyard, close to the graves of my unknown parents. And there my sister was laid quietly in the earth.

Biddy, Joe, and I had a cold dinner together. But we dined in the best parlor, not in the old kitchen. When evening closed in, I went into the garden with Biddy for a little talk.

"Biddy," said I, "I suppose it will be difficult for you to remain here now?"

"Oh! I can't do so, Mr. Pip," said Biddy, in a tone of **regret**.

"How are you going to live, Biddy? Do you want any money?"

"How am I going to live?" repeated Biddy, "I am going to try to get the place of teacher in the new school here."

SPECULATION (spek yuh <u>lay</u> shun) *n.*
the result of pondering about something
Synonyms: theory, guess, conjecture

DEFINITE (<u>def</u> uh nit) *adj.*
having distinct limits, well defined
Synonyms: certain, exact, clear

I nodded, and she then told me how Joe loved me and how Joe never complained of anything. "Are you quite sure, then, that you WILL come to see him often?" asked Biddy looking at me.

"Of course I will," I said.

Early in the morning I was to go. There I stood, looking at Joe, already at work.

"Good-bye, dear Joe! No, don't wipe it off! Give me your blackened hand! I shall be down soon and often."

"Never too soon, sir," said Joe, "and never too often, Pip!"

Once more, the mists were rising as I walked away.

I came back to Herbert, and he and I went on from bad to worse, increasing our debts. I came of age. We had looked forward to my one-and-twentieth birthday with a crowd of **speculations**, for we had both thought that my guardian could hardly help saying something **definite** on that occasion.

I received a note telling me that Mr.

DONOR (<u>doh</u> nur) *n.*

someone who gives something without asking
for anything in return
Synonyms: patron, benefactor, contributor

AFFAIR (uh <u>fair</u>) *n.*

commercial or personal business
Synonyms: matter, concern

Jaggers would be glad if I would call upon him at five in the afternoon of my birthday. This made us sure that something great was to happen, and I quickly arrived at my guardian's office.

"Well, Pip," said he, "I must call you Mr. Pip today. Congratulations, Mr. Pip."

"Is my benefactor to be made known to me today?"

"No."

"Have – I – anything to receive, sir?"

"Now, Mr. Pip," said Mr. Jaggers, "You are in debt, of course?"

"I am afraid I must say yes, sir."

He nodded and handed me something. "This is a <u>bank-note</u>," he said, "for five hundred pounds. That handsome sum of money, Pip, is your own. It is a present to you on this day. And at the rate of that handsome sum of money each year, and at no higher rate, you are to live until the **donor** of the whole appears. You will now take your money **affairs** into your own hands, and you will draw one hundred

PATRON (<u>pay</u> truhn) *n.*

a person who pays for another person's expenses

Synonyms: supporter, benefactor

SUMMON (<u>suhm</u> uhn) *v.* **-ing**, **-ed**

to request the presence of

Synonyms: call, hail

and twenty-five pounds per quarter until you are in communication with your benefactor."

After a pause, I said, "Is it likely that my **patron**, will soon come to London or **summon** me anywhere else?"

"What did I first tell you about your patron?" replied Mr. Jaggers, fixing me with his dark eyes.

"You told me, Mr. Jaggers, that it might be years until that person appeared."

"Just so," said Mr. Jaggers, "that's my answer. When that person appears, you and that person will settle your own affairs. Then my part in this business will end."

We looked at one another. All I could imagine was that Miss Havisham had not taken him into her confidence and that he did not know that she planned me for Estella. Or perhaps he knew and felt jealous or objected to the scheme.

Something great and wonderful had been done for me, and now I was determined to do something great and wonderful for my friend

ANONYMOUSLY (uh <u>non</u> uh muhss lee) *adv.*
done without revealing a name or identity
Synonyms: namelessly, unidentifiably

RADIANT (<u>ray</u> dee uhnt) *adj.*
shining
Synonyms: glowing, gleaming

TRIUMPH (<u>trye</u> uhmf) *n.*
a great victory or achievement
Synonym: success

Herbert Pocket. I knew he might have done better without me and my great expectations. I also knew that his pride would not let him take anything from me willingly. Now having money, I found a merchant who would one day be in need of a young partner, and I bought Herbert the partnership. I paid half the money and arranged to pay the rest at a later date. I arranged it all **anonymously**, so that Herbert did not know the identity of his benefactor.

Herbert had not the least suspicion of my hand being in it. I never shall forget his **radiant** face when he came home one afternoon, and told me a mighty piece of news. He said he had a job now with one Clarriker (the young merchant's name), and with prospects of a partnership later on. I had the greatest difficulty in stopping my tears of **triumph** when I saw him so happy. I did really cry when I went to bed, so happy that my expectations had done some good to somebody.

Shortly afterwards, I went to visit Estella

OPPOSED (uh <u>pozd</u>) *adj.*
taking differing sides or positions
Synonym: contrary

DETACH (di <u>tach</u>) *v.* **-ing**, **-ed**
to remove one part of something from the rest
of it
Synonyms: separate, disconnect, sever

RETORT (ri <u>tort</u>) *n.*
an answer that is given quickly or sharply
Synonyms: response, rejoinder

and Miss Havisham at the grim house, and it was the first time I had ever seen them **opposed**. We were seated by the fire. Miss Havisham clutched Estella's hand in hers, when Estella gradually began to **detach** herself. "What!" said Miss Havisham, flashing her eyes upon her, "are you tired of me?"

"Only a little tired of myself," replied Estella, looking down at the fire.

Miss Havisham struck her cane on the floor, "Speak the truth, you are tired of me! You cold, cold heart!"

"What?" said Estella, "do you scold me for being cold? You?"

"Are you not?" was the fierce **retort**.

"You should know," said Estella. "I am what you have made me. What would you have?"

"Love," replied the other.

"You have it."

"I have not," said Miss Havisham.

"Mother by adoption," retorted Estella, "you ask me to give you what you never gave me!"

ADMISSION (ad <u>mish</u> shun) *n.*
  the right to enter
      Synonyms: acceptance, entrance

EXCLUDE (eks <u>klood</u>) *v.* **-ing**, **-ed**
  to prevent from entering
      Synonyms: leave out, forbid, disallow

"Did I never give her love!" cried Miss Havisham, turning wildly to me.

"Who knows you as well as I do?" asked Estella. "I sat learning your lessons and looking up into your face, when your face was strange and frightened me. When have you found me false to your teaching? When have you found me unmindful of your lessons? When have you found me giving **admission** here," she touched her chest with her hand, "to anything that you **excluded**?"

"So proud!" moaned Miss Havisham.

"Who taught me to be proud?" returned Estella. "Who taught me to be hard?"

"But to be proud and hard to me!" Miss Havisham shrieked.

Estella looked at her with calm wonder. "I have never forgotten your wrongs and their causes. I have always followed your schooling. I must be taken as I have been made."

Miss Havisham sank to the floor. I gave Estella a look begging her to go to Miss Havisham. But as I left, Estella was standing

ADRIFT (uh <u>drift</u>) *adj.*
floating freely, without purpose or direction
Synonyms: loose, drifting

away from her, just as she had stood throughout. Miss Havisham's gray hair was all **adrift** upon the ground, and was a miserable sight to see.

ENLIGHTEN (en <u>lite</u> uhn) *v.* **-ing**, **-ed**
to help someone understand
Synonyms: teach, instruct

FOLLY (<u>fol</u> ee) *n.*
a lack of good sense
Synonyms: silliness, absurdity, nonsense

CHAPTER 8

I was twenty-three years old. Not another word had I heard to **enlighten** me about my expectations. We had left Barnard's Inn more than a year ago, and now lived in a place called the Temple.

One evening, I was reading, when I heard footsteps. Nervous **folly** made me jump at the sound. I ran to look down the staircase, but

VOYAGER (<u>voi</u> ij ur) *n.*

a person who is on a journey
Synonyms: traveler, wayfarer

EXPOSURE (ek <u>spohz</u> zhur) *n.*

the state of being uncovered or without
protection
Synonyms: vulnerability, defenselessness

ASCEND (uh <u>send</u>) *v.* **-ing, -ed**

to move up
Synonyms: climb, rise, mount

AMAZEMENT (uh <u>maze</u> ment) *n.*

the state of being very surprised, the seeing of
something unusual or extraordinary
Synonyms: astonishment, wonder

saw nothing but dark. Is there someone down there?" I called.

"Yes," said a voice from the darkness.

"What floor do you want?"

"The top. Mr. Pip."

"That is my name. There is nothing the matter?"

"Nothing the matter," returned the voice.

I stood with my lamp held out over the stair-rail, and he came slowly within its light. In the instant, I had seen a face that was strange to me, looking up with an air of being touched and pleased by the sight of me.

I made out that he was dressed roughly, like a sea **voyager**. He had long iron-gray hair and was about sixty, browned and hardened by **exposure** to weather. As he **ascended** the last stair or two, I saw, with **amazement**, that he was holding out both his hands to me.

Suddenly I knew him! He was my convict from the churchyard where we first stood face to face when I was but a boy! Not knowing

NOBLE (<u>noh</u> buhl) *adj.*
    acting with great concern, of a high nature
        Synonyms: honorable, gallant, high-minded

MENDING (<u>men</u> ding) *n.*
    the act of repairing or making something better
        Synonyms: fixing, restoring

RENEW (ri <u>noo</u>) *v.* **-ing**, **-ed**
    to begin again
        Synonyms: revive, restart

what to do, I gave him my hands. He kissed them and still held them.

"You acted **noble**, my boy," said he. "And I have never forgot it!"

"If you are grateful to me for what I did when I was a little child, I hope you have shown your thankfulness by **mending** your way of life. If you have come here to thank me, it was not necessary," I cried. "But I cannot wish to **renew** that chance acquaintance with you of long ago. But you are wet, and you look tired. Will you drink something before you go?"

I saw with amazement that his eyes were full of tears.

"How are you living?" I asked him.

"I've been a sheep-farmer and other trades besides. I've done wonderfully well."

"Like you, I have done well, and you must let me pay the two one-pound notes you once had someone bring me. You can put them to some other poor boy's use." I took out my wallet.

He watched me as I opened my wallet upon the table. I took out two one-pound notes and

FALTER (<u>fawl</u> tur) *v.* **-ing**, **-ed**
to move or act in an unsteady way
Synonym: hesitate

CONSEQUENCE (<u>kon</u> suh kwenss) *n.*
the outcome of an action
Synonyms: result, effect, repercussion

MULTITUDE (<u>muhl</u> ti tood) *n.*
a great number of people or things
Synonyms: crowd, throng, swarm

handed them over to him. Still watching me, he folded them, gave them a twist, set fire to them at the lamp, and dropped the ashes into the tray.

"May I make so bold," he said then, with a smile that was like a frown, "as to ask you how you have done well, since you and me was out on them shivering marshes?"

I told him that I had a benefactor and I would get some property in the future.

"Might a mere warmint ask what and whose property?" said he.

I **faltered**, "I don't know." With my heart beating like a hammer, I rose from my chair.

"There ought to have been some guardian, or such-like, whiles you was a minor," he said. "Some lawyer, maybe. As to the first letter of that lawyer's name now. Would it be J?"

All the truth of my position came flashing on me. Its disappointments, dangers, **consequences** of all kinds, rushed in in such a **multitude** that I had to struggle for every breath I drew.

"And," he said, "as the employer of that

SHUDDER (<u>shuhd</u> ur) *v.* **-ing**, **-ed**
   to shake violently
      Synonyms: shiver, quiver, tremble

ABHORRENCE (ab <u>hor</u> enss) *n.*
   a strong dislike
      Synonyms: hatred, loathing

lawyer whose name might be Jaggers, he might have come over the sea to see you."

I could not have spoken one word, even if it had been to save my life. The room began to turn, and I stumbled. He caught me, drew me to the sofa. He drew the face that I now well remembered, and that I **shuddered** at, near mine.

"Yes, Pip, dear boy, I've made a gentleman on you! It's me wot done it! I swore that sure as ever I earned a guinea, that guinea should go to you. I swore that if I got rich, you should get rich. I lived rough, so you should live smooth."

The **abhorrence** in which I held the man, the dread I had of him, could not have been more if he had been some terrible beast.

"Look'ee here, Pip. I've put away money for you. But didn't you never think it might be me?"

"Oh, no, no, no," I returned, "Never, never!"

"Well, you see it wos me. Never a soul in it but my own self and Mr. Jaggers. And, dear boy, how good looking you have growed! Isn't there bright eyes somewheres, wot you love the thoughts on?"

Oh, Estella, Estella!

COMPARISON (kuhm <u>pahr</u> uh sun) *n.*
the act of examining the similarities and
differences between two things
Synonyms: judgment, relating

ABSENT (<u>ab</u> suhnt) *adj.*
not present
Synonyms: away, missing, gone

CAUTION (<u>kaw</u> shun) *n.*
careful thought or action in order to
minimize risk
Synonyms: watchfulness, prudence

"Who you love shall be yours, dear boy, if money can buy 'em."

Oh that he had never come! That he had left me at the forge, far from contented, yet, by **comparison** happy!

"Where will you put me to sleep?" he asked, "for I've been sea-tossed and sea-washed, months and months."

"Herbert, my friend and companion," said I, rising from the sofa, "is **absent**. You must have his room."

"He won't come back tomorrow, will he? Because, dear boy," he said, dropping his voice, "**Caution** is necessary. I was <u>sent for life</u>. It's death to come back. I should be hanged if I was took by the law."

The wretched man had risked his life to come to me!

My first care was to close the <u>shutters</u>, so that no light might be seen from without, and then to close the doors. While I did so, he stood at the table drinking rum and eating biscuits, and when I saw him, I saw my convict on the marshes at

STOOP (stoop) *v.* **-ing**, **-ed**
to crouch down
Synonym: bend, hunch, squat

CONCEALED (kuhn <u>seeld</u>) *adj.*
out of sight
Synonyms: hidden, unseen, secreted

UNEXPECTEDLY (uhn ek <u>spek</u> tid lee) *adv.*
in a surprising way
Synonyms: accidentally, fortuitously

his meal again. It almost seemed to me as if he must **stoop** down to file at his leg.

Miss Havisham's intentions towards me were all a mere dream! Estella was not meant for me! I had been only a convenience, a model with a heart to practice on. But what brought the sharpest and deepest pain of all was that I had deserted Joe for the convict.

I could not go back to Joe now, I would not go to Biddy. My worthless conduct to them made it difficult to think about.

It was impossible to keep the convict **concealed** in the rooms. The attempt to do it would surely make people suspicious. I planned to announce that my uncle had **unexpectedly** come from the country.

The next morning, my convict looked worse than ever. "I do not even know," said I, speaking low as he took his seat at the table, "by what name to call you. I will tell people that you are my uncle."

"That's it! Call me uncle. I took the name Provis on ship. Call me that if you need to."

"What is your real name?" I asked.

FLOURISH (<u>flur</u> ish) *n.*

a grand movement with the hand

Synonyms: gesture, sweep, twist

FRENZY (<u>fren</u> zee) *n.*

a state of being wildly excited

Synonyms: outburst, agitation

"Magwitch," he answered, "Abel."

"What were you brought up to be?"

"A warmint, dear boy."

"Are you known in London?"

"I hope not!" said he.

"Were you – tried – in London?"

"Which time?" said he, with a sharp look.

"The last time."

He nodded. "First knowed Mr. Jaggers that way. Jaggers took my case to court."

It was on my lips to ask him what he was tried for, but he took up a knife, gave it a **flourish**, and with the words, "What I done is now paid for!" fell to his breakfast.

After he ate, he took out of his pocket a great thick wallet, bursting with papers, and tossed it on the table.

"It's yourn. There's more where that come from. I've come to the old country fur to see my gentleman spend his money like a gentleman. That'll be my pleasure."

"Stop!" said I, in a **frenzy** of fear and dislike, "I want to know how you are to be kept out of

INFORM (in <u>form</u>) *v.* **-ing**, **-ed**
   to reveal information to another person
      Synonyms: tell, advise

DISGUISING (diss <u>gize</u> ing) *adj.*
   changing one's appearance
      Synonym: camouflaging

SECURE (si <u>kyure</u>) *v.* **-ing**, **-ed**
   to get
      Synonyms: obtain, procure

danger, how long you are going to stay, how we can keep you from being recognized and seized?"

"Well, dear boy, the danger ain't so great. There's Jaggers, and there's you who know I am here. Who else could **inform** on me?"

"Is there no chance person who might know you in the street?" said I.

"Well," he returned, "There ain't many. If the danger had been fifty times as great, I should ha' come to see you, mind you, just the same."

"And how long do you remain?"

"I'm not going back. I've come for good."

"Where are you to live?" said I. "What is to be done with you? Where will you be safe?"

"Dear boy," he returned, "there's **disguising** wigs can be bought for money, and spectacles, and there's black clothes."

"You take it smoothly now," said I, "but you were very serious last night, when you swore it was death."

"And so I swear it is death by the rope," said he, "But here I am. For you."

The next day, I **secured** for him – as my

FLEE (flee) *v.* **-ing, fled**
   to leave quickly
      Synonyms: run away, abscond, escape

uncle, Mr. Provis – some quiet lodging near by in a respectable rooming house in Essex Street. I then went from shop to shop, buying what things were necessary to change his appearance. Then I went to see Mr. Jaggers at Little Britain.

Mr. Jaggers was at his desk, but, seeing me enter, got up immediately.

"Now, Pip," said he, "Be careful."

"I merely want, Mr. Jaggers," said I, "to make sure that what I have been told is true. I have been informed by a person named Abel Magwitch that he is my benefactor."

"That is the man," said Mr. Jaggers, "in New South Wales, in Australia. And only he."

"I always believed it was Miss Havisham."

"I am not at all responsible for that," said Mr. Jaggers coolly.

We shook hands, and I left.

I spent time with my convict that evening. Every hour my abhorrence of him grew. I even think I might have **fled** from him. Once, I actually did start out of bed in the night, hurriedly planning to leave him there with everything else

ENLIST (en <u>list</u>) *v.* **-ing**, **-ed**
> to engage oneself in a service or task
> Synonyms: join, sign up, enroll

I owned, and **enlist** as a soldier in India. But I did not because of all he had done for me and the risk he ran and for the knowledge that Herbert would soon come back.

BREED (breed) *v.* **-ing**, **bred**
to bring up to be or do something
Synonyms: raised, nurtured

FOREIGN (<u>for</u> uhn) *adj.*
from or having to do with a different country
Synonyms: alien, distant, unfamiliar

INDUCE (in <u>dooss</u>) *v.* **-ing**, **-ed**
to persuade someone to do something
Synonyms: convince, coax

CHAPTER 9

Herbert shortly returned, and I told him all. "Think what I owe him already!" I said. "I am heavily in debt. I have no expectations. I have been **bred** to no calling. But I can take nothing more from him. Ever. Not a penny."

"The first thing to be done," said Herbert, "is to get him out of England. We must find some boat bound for **foreign** shores. He may be **induced** to go if you go with him."

TEND (tend) *v.* **-ing**, **-ed**
    to take care of
        Synonym: attend to

COMRADE (<u>kom</u> rad) *n.*
    a person often seen in the company of another
        Synonyms: companion, associate, friend

HANDY (<u>han</u> dee) *adj.*
    easy to do or to understand
        Synonyms: convenient, easy

"But get him where I will, could I stop his coming back?"

"You are bound to have that tenderness for the life he has risked on your account, to feel that you must save him from throwing it away. You must get him out of England first. That done, we will both try to **tend** to your life!"

I agreed and took him to meet Magwitch, who stood when he saw us. "This is my friend," I told him. "And he shall be a friend to you," I said. "He is on oath and will say nothing."

"I told my friend of what happened on the marshes, when we first met. Can you tell us more?"

"Well!" he said, after consideration. "You're on your oath, you know, Pip's **comrade**? To say nothing?"

"Assuredly," replied Herbert.

"Dear boy and Pip's comrade," said Magwitch. "I am going to give it you short and **handy**. In jail and out of jail. That's my life pretty much.

"Twenty years ago, I met a man. His name was Compeyson and that's the man what you saw me pounding in that ditch in the marshes.

SWINDLING (<u>swin</u> duhl ing) *n.*
taking someone's property by trickery
Synonyms: cheating, defrauding, fleecing

FORGING (<u>forj</u> ing) *n.*
making illegal copies of something
Synonyms: imitating, copying

"He pretended to be a gentleman, this Compeyson. Compeyson took me on to be his partner. Compeyson's business was **swindling**, **forging**, stealing, and such. There was another in with Compeyson, as was called Arthur. Him and Compeyson had been in a bad thing with a rich lady some years afore, and they'd made a pot of money by it. But Compeyson betted and gambled on everything, and he'd have run through the king's taxes. So, Arthur was dying poor and seeing fearful sights in his head.

"Arthur lived at the top of Compeyson's house. The second or third time as ever I see him, he come running into Compeyson's parlor late at night, in only a nightgown, with his hair all in a sweat, and he says to Compeyson's wife, 'Sally, she is upstairs and I can't get rid of her. She's all in white, and she's mad, and she's got a shroud and she says she'll put it on me at five in the morning.'

"Says Compeyson: 'Why, you fool, don't you know she's got a living body? And how should she be up there, without coming through the door, or in at the window, and up the stairs?'

FELONY (<u>fell</u> uhn ee) *n.*
   a serious illegal action
      Synonyms: offense, crime

CIRCULATION (sur kyuh <u>lay</u> shuhn) *n.*
   an orderly movement, the passage of something
   from one place to another
      Synonyms: flow, transmission

SEPARATE (<u>sep</u> ur it) *adj.*
   set or kept apart
      Synonyms: divided, alone, individual

DEFENSE (di <u>fenss</u>) *n.*
   the act of protecting oneself or something else,
   an action taken against an opponent
      Synonyms: protection, resistance, reply,
      argument

EVIDENCE (<u>ev</u> uh duhnss) *n.*
   something that proves or establishes the truth
      Synonyms: proof, fact, confirmation

"'I don't know how she's there,' says Arthur, shivering, 'but she's standing in the corner at the foot of the bed. And over where her heart's broke – you broke it! – there's drops of blood.'

"'Go up with this sick man,' Compeyson says to his wife, 'and Magwitch, lend her a hand, will you?' Then Arthur lifted himself up, fell, and was dead.

"Compeyson took it easy as a good riddance for both sides. Him and me was soon busy.

"I was always in debt to him, always getting into danger. My Missis as I had the hard time wi' – Stop though! I ain't brought her in—"

He looked about him in a confused way, and he turned his face to the fire.

"The time wi' Compeyson was a'most as hard a time as ever I had," he said. "Me and Compeyson was both committed for **felony,** on a charge of putting stolen bank notes in **circulation**. Compeyson says to me, '**Separate defenses**, no communication,' and that was all. When the **evidence** was given in the box, I noticed how it was always me that was blamed, it was always

VERDICT (ver <u>dikt</u>) *n.*
> the judgment in a trial
>> Synonyms: decision, outcome, ruling

MERCY (mer <u>cee</u>) *n.*
> lenient or caring treatment
>> Synonyms: compassion, charity, clemency

ASHORE (uh <u>shor</u>) *adv.*
> off the water and onto the nearby land
>> Synonym: aground

me that the money had been paid to. And when the **verdict** come, warn't it Compeyson who got **mercy** because of good character and bad company. And giving up all the information he could against me, warn't it me as got never a word but Guilty? And when I says to Compeyson, 'Once out of this court, I'll smash that face of yourn!' ain't it Compeyson as prays the judge to be protected, and gets two jailers stood between us? And when we're sentenced, ain't it him as gets seven year, and me fourteen?"

"We was in the same prison-ship, and at last I come behind him and hit him in the face hard. I was seen and seized. But I escaped the ship to the shore, and I was hiding among the graves there, when I first see my boy!"

He gave me a look of joy.

"By my boy, I was given to understand as Compeyson was out on them marshes too. I believe he escaped in his terror, to get rid of me, not knowing it was me as had got **ashore**. I hunted him down. I smashed his face. 'And

TOW (<u>toe</u>) *v.* **-ing, -ed**
　to pull along behind
　　Synonyms: drag, haul

CHILLED (chilld) *adj.*
　made cold by weather, fear, or worry
　　Synonyms: frigid, shocked, numbed

now,' says I 'as the worst thing I can do, caring nothing for myself, I'll drag you back.' And I'd have been **towing** him by the hair, if the soldiers hadn't got us first."

"Of course, his punishment was light. I was put in irons, brought to trial, and sent for life."

"Is Compeyson dead?" I asked.

He said with a fierce look. "I never heard no more of him."

Just then Herbert slid a note to me. It read: "Young Havisham's name was Arthur. Compeyson is the man Miss Havisham's loved!"

Chilled, I nodded slightly to Herbert, but we neither of us said anything, and both looked at Magwitch as he stood smoking by the fire.

ABROAD (uh <u>brawd</u>) *adv.*
away from one's home, in another country
Synonym: overseas

CHAPTER 10

Never would I breathe a word of Estella to Magwitch. But before I could go **abroad** with Magwitch, I knew I must see both Estella and Miss Havisham one last time!

In the room where the candles burnt on the wall, I found Miss Havisham seated on a couch near the fire, and Estella on a cushion at her feet, knitting at some wool. "And what wind," said Miss Havisham, "blows you here, Pip?"

"I have found out who my patron is. It is not

WHIM (wim) *n.*
a sudden idea
Synonyms: fancy, notion, caprice

BROOD (brood) *v.* **-ing**, **-ed**
to think in a gloomy or worried way
Synonyms: sulk, fret

a fortunate discovery. It is not my secret, but another's. I wish I had never left my village. When you first had me brought here, Miss Havisham, you had me come as a kind of servant, to satisfy a **whim**, and you paid me for it."

"Ay, Pip," replied Miss Havisham, "that's correct."

"And Mr. Jaggers—"

"Mr. Jaggers," said Miss Havisham, in a firm tone, "had nothing to do with it, and knew nothing of it. His being my lawyer, and his being the lawyer of your patron is a coincidence."

"But when I fell into the mistake I have so long remained in, you still led me on?" said I.

"Yes," she returned, "I let you go on."

"Was that kind?"

"Who am I, that I should be kind?" cried Miss Havisham, striking the ground with her cane so suddenly that Estella glanced up at her in surprise. She sat **brooding** after this outburst.

"I have asked these questions only for my own information," I said.

"Well, well, what else?" she said, calming.

RELATION (ruh <u>lay</u> shuhn) *n.*
someone who is connected by blood
Synonyms: family, kin, connection

ABILITY (uh <u>bil</u> i tee) *n.*
the state of being able to do something
successfully
Synonyms: skill, capacity, expertise

COMMAND (kuh <u>mand</u>) *v.* **-ing**, **-ed**
to have control over
Synonyms: control, govern

"I have been thrown among one family of your **relations**. Herbert Pocket, the son of my first tutor, Matthew Pocket. He is my dearest friend."

She studied me. "What do you want?"

"If you would spare the money to do my friend a lasting service, without telling him you are doing it, I should be grateful."

"Why do it without telling him?"

"Because I began it two years ago myself, without his knowledge and I don't want to be betrayed. Why I fail in my **ability** to finish it, I cannot say. It is part of someone else's secret."

She said she would think on it, and then I turned to Estella.

"Estella," said I, trying to **command** my trembling voice, "You know that I have loved you long and dearly. I had hoped that Miss Havisham meant us for one another."

Estella shook her head.

"I know," said I, "I have no hope that I shall ever call you mine, Estella. I don't know what may become of me very soon, how poor I may be, or

TORTURE (<u>tor</u> chur) *v.* **-ing, -ed**

to cause someone intense suffering
Synonyms: torment, hurt, abuse

VAIN (vayn) *adj.*

1. of no real value, with no hope of success
Synonyms: foolish, futile
2. thinking too highly of oneself
Synonyms: egotistical, conceited

REFLECT (ri <u>flekt</u>) *v.* **-ing, -ed**

to think seriously about something
Synonyms: consider, deliberate

FATAL (<u>fay</u> tuhl) *adj.*

causing deadly harm
Synonym: lethal

where I may go. Still, I love you. I have loved you since I first saw you in this house."

Her fingers were busy knitting some yarn. She shook her head again.

"Miss Havisham, you have been **torturing** me all these years with a **vain** hope. But I can't think you have **reflected** on what you did. I think that, in the endurance of your own trial, you forgot my trials."

Miss Havisham put her hand to her heart and held it there. She looked at Estella and at me.

"I am going to be married to another," said Estella.

I was able to control myself better than I could have expected, considering what agony it gave me to hear her say those words. When I raised my face again, there was such a terrible look upon Miss Havisham's face, that it stopped me in my hurry and grief.

"Estella, dearest Estella, do not let Miss Havisham lead you into this **fatal** step!" I cried. Estella looked at me with wonder. Miss Havisham, her hand still covering her heart, stared in pity and remorse.

CONVERSATION (kon ver <u>say</u> shuhn) *n.*
discussion
Synonyms: dialogue, communication

OVERLOOK (<u>oh</u> vur look) *v.* **-ing**, **-ed**
1. to look out over
Synonyms: view, oversee
2. to fail to notice
Synonyms: ignore, miss

DWELLING (<u>dwel</u> ing) *n.*
a place where someone lives
Synonyms: home, abode, domicile

Yet, this was not the only terrible time I had. Shortly after visiting Estella and Miss Havisham, I ran into Wemmick. He was a clerk from Jagger's office, a man who had befriended me and who knew from Jagger's that Magwitch was around. He took it upon himself to tell me, his voice low, that he had heard some **conversations** of late. He had discovered that Compeyson was about, too, and even worse, he was watching me and pursuing Magwitch!

Herbert had thought it best to hide Magwitch at a friend's home, which **overlooked** the river. When we were ready to leave by water, it would take hardly any time at all to get Magwitch to the proper place.

We had decided that we should not see one another until we were ready to leave. But I had to tell Herbert that Compeyson was about, and because he was in danger I wanted to see Magwitch. I immediately found and told Herbert and then we went to Magwitch's **dwelling**. I was surprised at the concern and tenderness I felt for Magwitch. I did not want him to worry

VANISH (<u>van</u> ish) *v.* **-ing, -ed**
>to make oneself unseen
>>Synonyms: disappear, fade away, leave

REASONABLE (<u>ree</u> zuhn uh buhl) *adj.*
>sensible, not extreme
>>Synonyms: judicious, advisable, fair

VENTURE (<u>ven</u> chur) *n.*
>an activity that is risky
>>Synonyms: adventure, enterprise

about Compeyson, so I did not tell him that his enemy had come back. Instead, I told him that we had to **vanish**.

"We must leave, the two of us," I told Magwitch, and for a moment, I felt such a flood of feeling that I thought of staying with him for good when we had left this place.

Magwitch was very **reasonable**. His coming back was a **venture**, he said, and he would do nothing to make it a desperate venture, and he had very little fear of his safety with such good help.

Herbert and I, both being good with boats, planned to take Magwitch down the river ourselves when the right time came. A boat would be hired for the purpose, without sailors. That would save at least a chance of suspicion. We agreed I should keep a boat at the Temple stairs and that I should start a habit of rowing. That way no one would notice when we finally rowed away. There were steamboats coming down the Thames bound for other countries, and when things felt safer, we could meet up with them.

I liked this scheme, and Magwitch was quite

ELATED (uh <u>lay</u> tid) *adj.*
    having or being in high spirits
        Synonyms: joyful, happy

EXECUTION (eks uh <u>kyu</u> shuhn) *n.*
    the process of carrying out a plan or deed
        Synonyms: completion, fulfillment, operation

CLASP (klassp) *v.* **-ing**, **-ed**
    to hold on tightly
        Synonyms: grab, clamp, grasp, grip

FRAUD (frawd) *n.*
    an act of deception or misrepresentation
        Synonyms: sham, cheat, hoax, trick

elated by it. We agreed that it should be carried into **execution**.

"I don't like to leave you here," I said to Magwitch, "though I cannot doubt your being safer here than near me. Good-bye!"

"Dear boy," he answered, **clasping** my hands, "I don't know when we may meet again, and I don't like good-bye. Say good-night!"

"Good-night! Herbert will go regularly between us, and when the time comes you may be certain I shall be ready!"

Next day I went to get the boat. It was brought round to the Temple stairs, and lay where I could reach it within a minute or two. Then, I began to go out as if for training and practice. Sometimes I went alone, sometimes I went with Herbert. I was often out in cold, rain, and sleet, but nobody took much note of me after I had been out a few times.

Some weeks passed without bringing any change. I was pressed for money by more than one creditor. But I had quite determined that it would be a heartless **fraud** to take more money from my

CONSTANT (<u>kohn</u> stuhnt) *adj.*
marked by firm resolution, being firm of mind,
opinion, or faith
Synonyms: fixed, steady, consistent

SUSPENSE (suh <u>spenss</u>) *n.*
a state of mental uncertainty
Synonym: apprehension

SOLITUDE (<u>sol</u> uh tood) *n.*
the state of being by oneself
Synonyms: isolation, seclusion

patron. And as the time wore on, I began to feel that Estella was married.

It was an unhappy life that I lived. Still, no new cause for fear arose. In **constant suspense**, I rowed about in my boat, and I waited, waited, waited for the right time to leave.

One cold evening, I thought I would comfort myself with dinner at once, and as I had hours of **solitude** before me if I went home to the Temple, I thought I would afterwards go to a theater for a play. There I saw Mr. Wopsle, who had been the church clerk in my old country town, a man who had been there when I was a child and the two convicts had been arrested. He approached me after the show was over.

"I thought he was with you, Mr. Pip, till I saw that you didn't notice him sitting behind you like a ghost."

"Who?" I said.

My former chill crept over me again.

"You remember when you were a child, and I dined at Gargery's, and some soldiers came to the door to get a pair of handcuffs fixed?"

SCUFFLE (<u>skuhf</u> uhl) *n.*
a struggle at close quarters
Synonym: fight

"I remember it very well."

"And you remember that there was a chase after two convicts? And that we joined in and found the two in a ditch? And there was a **scuffle** between them, and one of them had been much hurt about the face by the other?"

"I see it all before me now."

"Well, one of those two prisoners sat behind you tonight. I saw him over your shoulder."

"Steady!" I thought. I asked him then, "Which of the two do you suppose you saw?"

"The one who had been hurt," he answered.

"This is very curious!" said I, pretending it was nothing. We said our good-byes and then I rushed home, in terror, to warn Herbert that Compeyson was shadowing me "like a ghost."

PRUDENT (<u>prood</u> uhnt) *adj.*
marked by wisdom or carefulness
Synonyms: wise, smart, judicious

ENGAGEMENT (en <u>gayj</u> muhnt) *n.*
an arrangement to meet or do something at a
certain time
Synonym: appointment

RENDER (<u>ren</u> dur) *v.* **-ing, -ed**
1. to cause to be
   Synonym: make
2. to transfer to another
   Synonym: deliver
3. to give in return
   Synonym: repay

CHAPTER 11

In the middle of all my fear, Mr. Jaggers had me to dinner. I felt it **prudent** to go, plus I was curious why he wanted to see me.

There, at dinner, he told me that Miss Havisham wanted to see me about some business I had mentioned. I knew what business it was. It was the money for Herbert's partnership.

"I have an **engagement**," said I, "that **renders**

GLIDE (glide) *v.* **-ing, -ed**
   to move smoothly
      Synonyms: walk, slide

SEEK (seek) *v.* **-ing, sought**
   to search for
      Synonyms: look, hunt

me uncertain of my time. But I will try to go at once."

Just then the housekeeper entered. "Now, Molly, how slow you are today!" he said.

She was at his elbow when he addressed her. As she withdrew her hands, a certain action of her fingers caught my attention.

The action of her fingers was like the action of knitting. Her look was very intent. Surely, I had seen exactly such eyes and such hands on another occasion lately!

He told her to leave, and she **glided** out of the room. But she remained before me as plainly as if she were still there. I looked at those hands and eyes and flowing hair, and I compared them with other hands, other eyes, other hair that I knew. I looked again at those fingers with their knitting action. And I felt certain that this woman was Estella's mother.

I knew this was not the time to ask Jaggers for proof of this, nor did I imagine he might give it to me. But after we dined, I went to Jaggers' office to **seek** out his clerk, Wemmick, who was friendly

ACQUIT (uh <u>kwit</u>) *v.* **-ing**, **-ed**
to discharge, to find innocent
Synonyms: release, let go

to me. I wanted to see if he might tell me something about the housekeeper.

"Ah, Molly," Wemmick said. "She is a wild beast tamed."

"How did Mr. Jaggers tame her, Wemmick?"

"That's his secret. She has been with him many a long year."

"I wish you would tell me her story. You know that what is said between you and me goes no further."

Wemmick nodded and began to talk. "Years ago Molly was tried for murder and **acquitted**. She was a very handsome young woman."

"But she was acquitted."

"Mr. Jaggers was her lawyer," pursued Wemmick, with a look full of meaning, "It was a hard case, and he was just starting out. He did the case so well that everyone admired him for it. It made him famous. The murdered person was a woman, a good ten years older than Molly, very much larger and stronger. It was a case of jealousy. This woman had been married very young

FURY (<u>fyoo</u> ree) *n.*
intense, violent anger
Synonyms: rage, ferocity, furor

IMPROBABILITY (im prob uh <u>bill</u> uh tee) *n.*
something which is not likely to happen
Synonym: unlikelihood

BRAMBLE (<u>bram</u> buhl) *n.*
a bush or shrub with sharp edges or points
Synonyms: thorns, stickers

REVENGE (ri <u>venj</u>) *v.* **-ing, -ed**
to get back at someone for something he or
she did
Synonyms: pay back, retaliate

CONVINCING (kuhn <u>vinss</u> ing) *adj.*
able to convince someone of something
Synonyms: believable, plausible

208

to a wandering man, and she was a jealous **fury**. The murdered woman was found dead in a barn. There had been a violent struggle. She was bruised and scratched and torn, and she had been held by the throat, at last, and choked. Now, there was no evidence to blame any person but Molly. Mr. Jaggers made his case on the **improbabilities** of her having been able to do it. He never dwelt upon the strength of her hands then, though he sometimes does now.

"Well, sir!" Wemmick went on, "it happened that this woman was so very carefully dressed that she looked much slighter than she really was, and her arms had a delicate look. She had only a bruise or two about her and scratches on her hands that Mr. Jaggers claimed were made from **brambles** and not from another person who might have been fighting her. She was also under strong suspicion of having destroyed her three-year-old child by this man to **revenge** herself upon him. But there was no evidence of a child. Mr. Jaggers was so **convincing** that the jury found Molly not guilty."

STUNNED (stuhnd) *adj.*
made senseless
Synonym: shocked

EXPRESSION (eks <u>presh</u> shun) *n.*
the emotions shown on someone's face
Synonyms: look, appearance, visage

"Has she been in his service ever since?"

"She went into his service immediately after her acquittal," said Wemmick, "tamed as she is now. She has since been taught one thing and another in the way of her duties, but she was tamed from the beginning."

"Do you remember the sex of the child?"

"Said to have been a girl."

I left Wemmick feeling **stunned**. I couldn't help but feel that Miss Havisham might have the final pieces of this puzzle, so I went to see her, as indeed, she had asked me to do.

When I got there, I saw that there was an air of utter loneliness upon her.

"It is I, Pip. Mr. Jaggers gave me your note yesterday, and I have lost no time."

"Thank you. Thank you."

As I brought a ragged chair near her and sat, I saw a new **expression** on her face, as if she were afraid of me.

"I want," she said, "to pursue that subject you mentioned to me when you were last here, and to show you that I am not all stone. But perhaps

REASSURING (ree uh <u>shur</u> ing) *adj.*
restoring confidence
Synonym: calming, restorative

RECALL (ri <u>kawl</u>) *v.* **-ing**, **-ed**
1. to call back, to bring back to mind
Synonyms: return, remember
2. to revoke
Synonym: cancel

TRANSACTION (tran <u>zak</u> shuhn) *n.*
an exchange of goods or service
Synonyms: business, trade

you can never believe, now, that there is anything human in my heart?"

When I said some **reassuring** words, she stretched out her trembling right hand as though she was going to touch me, but she **recalled** it again.

"You said, speaking for your friend, Herbert, that I could do something useful and good. Can you explain it again and further?"

I explained to her the secret history of the partnership I had planned for Herbert. I told her how I had been unable to complete the **transaction** with my own money.

"So!" said she, not looking at me. "How much money is needed to complete the transaction?"

I was rather afraid of saying it, for it sounded a large sum. "Nine hundred pounds."

"If I do this, will you keep my giving the money a secret? The same way you have kept your own secret?"

"Quite as faithfully."

"And your mind will be more at rest?"

BLIGHTED (<u>blite</u> ed) *adj.*
   injured or damaged
      Synonyms: ruined, destroyed

TABLET (<u>tab</u> lit) *n.*
   bound paper to write on
      Synonym: pad

"Much more at rest."

"Are you very unhappy now?"

She asked this question, still without looking at me but in a tone of sympathy. I could not reply at the moment, for my voice failed me. She put her left arm across the head of her cane and softly laid her forehead on it.

"I am far from happy, Miss Havisham, but I have other causes and other secrets."

She raised her head and looked at the fire.

"It is good of you to tell me that you have other causes of unhappiness. Is it true?"

"Too true."

"Can I only serve you, Pip, by serving your friend? Considering that as done, is there nothing I can do for you yourself?"

"I thank you for the question. But there is nothing."

She rose from her seat, and looked about the **blighted** room. Then she took from her pocket a yellow set of ivory **tablets** and wrote upon them with a pencil.

RECEIPT (ri <u>seet</u>) *n.*

    1. the act of receiving
      Synonyms: obtain, get
    2. a written notice acknowledging that
    something has been received
      Synonyms: note, mark

KNEEL (<u>neel</u>) *v.* **-ing**, **-ed** or **knelt**
    to lower oneself to the knees
      Synonyms: bend, bow

"You are still on friendly terms with Mr. Jaggers?"

"Quite. I dined with him yesterday."

"This is an authority to him to pay you that money for your friend. But if you would rather Mr. Jaggers knew nothing of the matter, I will send the money to you myself."

"Thank you, Miss Havisham. I have not the least objection to receiving it from him."

She read me what she had written. It was direct and clear and intended to clear me from any suspicion of gaining by the **receipt** of the money myself. I took the tablets from her hand, and then she took the pencil and handed it to me. All this she did without looking at me.

"My name is there. If you can ever write under my name, 'I forgive her,' though ever so long after my broken heart is dust, pray do it!"

"Miss Havisham," said I, "I can do it now."

To see her with her white hair and her worn face gave me a shock. She **kneeled** at my feet. I begged her to rise and got my arms about her to help her up. She pressed my hand and wept.

DESPAIRINGLY (di <u>spair</u> ing lee) *adv.*
without hope
Synonyms: hopelessly, forlornly,
despondently

INJURE (<u>in</u> jur) *v.* **-ing**, **-ed**
to cause harm, to inflict pain
Synonyms: hurt, damage, impair

WRING (ring) *v.* **-ing**, **wrung**
to squeeze or clasp and unclasp
Synonyms: twist, squirm

IMPRESSIONABLE (im <u>presh</u> uhn nuh buhl) *adj.*
easily impressed or moved
Synonyms: influenceable, swayable

I had never seen her cry before, and, in the hope that the crying might do her good, I bent over her without speaking. She was now down upon the ground.

"Oh!" she cried, **despairingly**. "What have I done!"

"If you mean, Miss Havisham, what have you done to **injure** me, let me answer. Very little. I should have loved her under any circumstances. Is she married?"

"Yes." She **wrung** her hands and cried over and over again. "What have I done!"

I knew not how to answer or how to comfort her. That she had done a terrible thing in taking an **impressionable** child to shape as she saw fit was beyond horrible. "Until you spoke to her the other day, and until I saw in you the same kind of pain and love for another that I once felt myself, I did not know what I had done. What have I done! What have I done!" And so again, twenty, fifty times over, What had she done!

"Miss Havisham," I said, when her cry had

SCRAP (skrap) *n.*
a small piece
Synonyms: bit, fragment

MISERY (<u>miz</u> uh ree) *n.*
a state of suffering or sadness
Synonyms: unhappiness, distress,
discomfort

PRAISE (prayz) *n.*
expression of approval
Synonyms: compliment, commendation

died away, "you may dismiss me from your mind. But Estella is a different case, and if you can ever undo any **scrap** of what you have done to her, it will be better to do that than to cry over the past for a hundred years."

"Yes, yes, I know it. But, Pip – my dear!" There was a true feeling and sorrow for me now. "Believe this. When she first came to me, I meant to save her from **misery** like my own. At first, I meant no more."

"Well, well!" said I. "I hope so."

"But as she grew and became very beautiful, I gradually did worse. With my **praises** and with my jewels and with my teachings. I was always before her, as a warning of what she might become if she was not careful. I stole her heart away, and put ice in its place."

"Better," I could not help saying, "to have left her a natural heart, even to be broken."

"If you knew all my story," she pleaded, "you would have some compassion for me and a better understanding of me."

"Miss Havisham," I answered, as delicately

INSPIRE (in <u>spire</u>) *v.* **-ing**, **-ed**
   to influence someone
      Synonyms: encourage, sway, affect

as I could, "I believe I may say that I do know your story, and have known it ever since I first left this neighborhood. It has **inspired** me to feel for you. Does what has passed between us give me any excuse for asking you a question about Estella? Not as she is, but as she was when she first came here?"

She slowly nodded, "Ask."

"Do you know whose child Estella was?"

She shook her head. "Mr. Jaggers brought her here."

"Will you tell me how that came about?"

She answered in a low whisper. "I had been shut up in these rooms a long time when I told him that I wanted a little girl to raise and love, and save from ending up as I did. He told me that he would look about him for such an orphan child. One night he brought her here asleep, and I called her Estella."

"Might I ask her age then?"

"Two or three years. She herself knows only that she was left an orphan and I adopted her."

PROLONGING (pruh <u>lawng</u> ing) *n.*

the process of making something longer

Synonyms: lengthening, extending

INTERVIEW (<u>in</u> tur vyoo) *n.*

a meeting, a conversation in which information is exchanged

Synonyms: consultation, exchange

BEHALF (bi <u>haf</u>) *n.*

interest

Synonyms: benefit, support

EASE (eez) *v.* **-ing**, **-ed**

1. to lessen pressure, to make less painful

Synonyms: alleviate, soothe

2. to move gently

Synonym: slip

TWILIGHT (<u>twye</u> lite) *n.*

the period between night and sunrise or between daytime and sunset

Synonyms: dawn, dusk

I was convinced now that Molly was her mother.

What more could I hope to do by **prolonging** the **interview**? I had succeeded on **behalf** of Herbert, Miss Havisham had told me all she knew of Estella, and I had said and done what I could to **ease** her mind. Gently, we parted.

Twilight was closing in when I went out the door. I had a feeling that I should never be there again.

I looked back into the room where I had left her, and I saw her seated in the ragged chair close to the fire, with her back towards me. Then, suddenly, I saw a great flaming light spring up. In the same moment, I saw her running at me, on fire and shrieking, with flames blazing and soaring all about her.

I had a heavy coat on. I got it off, threw her down, and got the coat over her, hoping to put out the fires. I dragged the cloth from the table for the same purpose, and with it dragged down all the rotten things that were set there. The more I covered her, the more wildly she shrieked and

TINDER (<u>tin</u> der) *n.*

substances that can easily burn or catch fire
Synonym: kindling

CONSUME (kuhn <u>soom</u>) *v.* **-ing**, **-ed**

to do away with completely
Synonyms: use up, eliminate, eat

tried to free herself. Then we were on the floor by the great table, and patches of **tinder** were floating in the smoky air.

She was not moving or speaking. I was afraid to have her moved or even touched. Assistance was sent for, and I held her until it came, as if I thought that if I let her go the fire would break out again and **consume** her. When the surgeon arrived, I got up, and I was astonished to see that both my hands were burnt.

Miss Havisham had received serious hurts, but they were far from hopeless. The danger lay in the nervous shock she had suffered. By the surgeon's directions, her bed was carried up onto the great table, which was well suited to the tending of her injuries. This was the same place she had once said she would lay one day.

I found, on questioning the servants, that Estella was in Paris, and I got a promise from the surgeon that he would write to her.

There was a moment that evening, when Miss Havisham spoke about what had happened. Towards midnight, she began to wander in her

SOLEMN (<u>sol</u> uhm) *adj.*
marked by seriousness
Synonyms: grave, somber

speech. She said over and over in a low **solemn** voice, "What have I done!" And then, "When she first came, I meant to save her from misery like mine." And then, "Take the pencil and write under my name, 'I forgive her', take the pencil and write under my name, 'I forgive her!'"

EXCEEDINGLY (eks <u>eed</u> ing lee) *adv.*
extremely
Synonym: very

FOND (fond) *adj.*
having a strong positive feeling for
Synonyms: attached, warm

STRANGLE (<u>strang</u> guhl) *v.* **-ing**, **-ed**
to squeeze someone's neck to stop their breath
Synonyms: choke, gag, throttle

CHAPTER 12

I came home, my hands still hurt, and Herbert took good care of me. I told him about Molly and how I believed Estella was her child, given to Miss Havisham. He listened and then he told me that he would tell me all that Magwitch had told him.

"Molly and Magwitch had a child!" he said. He said that Magwitch was **exceedingly fond** of the child. On the evening when the object of her jealousy was **strangled**, Molly went to Magwitch

GRIEVE (greeve) *v.* **-ing**, **-ed**
    to feel great sorrow
        Synonyms: mourn, lament

GENIUS (<u>jee</u> nee uhss *or* <u>jeen</u> yuhss) *n.*
    a person of great capacity, a person of
    unusually great intelligence
        Synonyms: master, star, wizard

TRAGICALLY (<u>traj</u> ik uh lee *or* traj ik lee) *adv.*
    in a sad way, leading to destruction
        Synonyms: disastrously, dreadfully

BOLT (bohlt) *v.* **-ing**, **-ed**
    to jump up without warning, to leave suddenly
        Synonyms: spring, start, leap

and swore that if he told what he knew about her jealousy and about that day of the murder, she would destroy the child and he should never see it again. Then, she vanished.

"Now," pursued Herbert, "Magwitch was afraid after that, and so he hid himself, even though he **grieved** for the child. He kept himself out of her trial. After she was acquitted, she disappeared. He couldn't help but believe the child was dead and that he lost the child and the child's mother."

"I want to ask—"

"A moment, my dear boy. Let me finish! That evil **genius**, Compeyson, was aware that Magwitch knew about Molly and why Magwitch had kept away from the trial. So he held that knowledge over Magwitch's head. It was his way of keeping him poorer and working him harder."

Herbert tended my wounds. "He said that when he first saw you, you brought into his mind the little girl so **tragically** lost, who would have been about your age."

I **bolted** upright. The pieces were all fitting together. "Herbert!" I cried. "That little girl is alive!

PRODUCE (pro <u>dooss</u>) *v.* **-ing, -ed**
   to bring forward
      Synonyms: show, present, exhibit

And the man we have in hiding down the river is Estella's father."

I now had two reasons to see Mr. Jaggers immediately. I had to find out what Mr. Jaggers knew of all this. And I had to give him Miss Havisham's authority for the money that would secure Herbert's partnership.

I went that very night, with my arm bandaged, and **produced** Miss Havisham's authority to receive the money for Herbert. Then I told him that I knew the identity of Estella's father.

"So! You know the young lady's father, Pip?" said Mr. Jaggers.

"Yes," I replied, "and his name is Magwitch from New South Wales." Then I told him all I knew, and how I came to know it. Mr. Jaggers stood quite still and silent.

"Now, Pip," said Mr. Jaggers, quietly. "I am not saying yes and I am not saying no. Instead I would have you imagine a story." Here, he took a deep breath. "Imagine a woman, under such circumstances as you have mentioned, and her having held her child concealed, and her being obliged

LEGAL (<u>lee</u> guhl) *adj.*
1. having to do with the law
2. conforming to the law
   Synonym: lawful

ADVISER (ad <u>vize</u> uhr) *n.*
someone who guides another person
   Synonyms: teacher, instructor, counsel

ATMOSPHERE (<u>at</u> muhss fihr) *n.*
1. the air in a given place
   Synonyms: air, sky
2. the general influences or environment of a place
   Synonyms: ambience, spirit

DESTRUCTION (di <u>struhk</u> shuhn) *n.*
the act of destroying or being destroyed
   Synonyms: ruin, devastation

IMPRISON (im <u>priz</u> uhn) *v.* **-ing, -ed**
to lock up in prison or jail
   Synonyms: jail, confine, incarcerate

to tell the fact to her **legal adviser**. Imagine that that advisor held a trust to find a child for a rich lady to adopt and bring up."

"I follow you, sir."

"Imagine that this lawyer lived in an **atmosphere** of evil, and that all he saw of children was their being led to certain **destruction**. Imagine that he often saw children **imprisoned**, whipped, forgotten, and growing up to be hanged."

"I follow you, sir."

"Now imagine, Pip, that here was one pretty little child who could be saved. Her father believed her dead and so dared make no noise about things. Imagine the power the legal adviser held over the mother. He knew what she did and how she did it. He told her to part with the child, to place the child in his hands, and he would do his best to save her. If the woman was saved, then her child was saved, too. If she was lost, then her child was still saved. Imagine that this was done, and that the woman was cleared."

"I understand you perfectly."

"But that I make no admissions?"

INKLING (ingk ling) *n.*
a vague idea or notion
Synonyms: hint, clue, glimmer

COMPREHEND (kom pri hend) *v.* **-ing, -ed**
to understand the meaning
Synonyms: fathom, grasp, perceive

IMAGINARY (i maj uh ner ee) *adj.*
made up, not existing in reality
Synonyms: fictitious, fabulous

SAKE (sayke) *n.*
the good or celebration of someone or
something else
Synonyms: honor, benefit

"I understand."

He nodded and continued. "Imagine that the terror of death had shaken the woman. When she was set at liberty, she was scared now by the ways of the world. So she went to that legal adviser to be sheltered. Imagine that he took her in and that he kept down the old, wild, violent nature whenever he saw an **inkling** of its breaking out. Do you **comprehend** the **imaginary** case?"

"Quite."

"Imagine that the child grew up, and was married for money. The mother was still living. The father was still living. In fact, the mother and father, unknown to one another, were living close to each other. The secret was still a secret, except that you had heard of it. Imagine that very carefully."

"I do."

"For who's **sake** would you reveal the secret? For the father's? I think he would not be much better off for knowing the mother was alive and how she might still try to hurt such a child. For the mother's? I think she would be safer where she

CONCLUDE (kon <u>clood</u>) *v.* **-ing**, **-ed**
to bring to an end
Synonyms: complete, finish

SLACKEN (<u>slak</u> en) *v.* **-ing**, **-ed**
to become slower or less intense, to loosen
Synonyms: lessen, decrease, ebb

URGENT (<u>ur</u> juhnt) *adj.*
demanding immediate action
Synonyms: vital, crucial, compelling

was. For the daughter's? I think it would hardly serve her to know who her parents were and to tell her husband. It would disgrace her."

We stood looking at one another, and I then had to agree with him. Shortly afterwards, I left with my money in my pocket, **concluding** the arrangement I had made in secret for Herbert. It was the only good thing I had done, and the only completed thing I had done since I was first told of my great expectations.

And now, indeed, I felt as if my last anchor were loosening its hold. We had now got into the month of March. Herbert and I both knew things had **slackened** enough so that it was now time to make our getaway with Magwitch.

"I have thought it over again and again," said Herbert, "and I think we should have some help. I know a man named Startop who can take us to a steamer. He is a good fellow, a skilled hand.

"It is necessary," Herbert went on, "to tell him very little until the morning comes. Then let him know that there is **urgent** reason for your getting Magwitch aboard and away."

CALCULATE (<u>kal</u> kyuh late) *v.* **-ing**, **-ed**
to determine by computation
Synonyms: compute, figure, reckon

INVESTIGATION (in <u>vess</u> tuh gay shuhn) *n.*
the process of examining or searching
Synonyms: search, exploration, inquiry

VESSEL (<u>vess</u> uhl) *n.*
1. a craft that travels over water
Synonyms: ship, boat
2. a hollow object used to hold something
Synonyms: receptacle, cup, pitcher, basin

PRECAUTION (pri <u>kaw</u> shuhn) *n.*
an action taken to protect against possible
difficulty or danger
Synonyms: safeguard, care

Any foreign ship that fell in our way and would take us up would do. As foreign steamers would leave London at about the time of high-water, our plan would be to get down the river by the time the tide turned. We would then wait in some quiet spot until we could get to one of the ships. The time when one would be due could be **calculated**, if we made inquiries beforehand.

We went out immediately after breakfast to pursue our **investigations**. We found that a steamer for Hamburg, Germany, was likely to suit our purpose best, and we directed our thoughts to that **vessel**.

We arranged that Herbert, Startop, and I should take the boat and go get Magwitch when the time was right. It was decided that we should prepare Magwitch ahead of time. Indeed, we would make all the arrangements with him by the night before, and he would be communicated with no more in any way until we took him on board.

When these **precautions** were well understood by both of us, I went home.

OBVIOUS (<u>ob</u> vee uhss) *adj.*
  easily seen, readily understood
    Synonyms: apparent, clear, evident, open

REFRAINING (ri <u>frayn</u> ing) *n.*
  the act of holding back
    Synonyms: abstaining, renunciation

SPANNED (spannd) *adj.*
  extended across
    Synonyms: crossed, covered

UTTERLY (<u>uht</u> ur lee) *adv.*
  completely
    Synonyms: absolutely, entirely

WHOLLY (<u>hol</u> lee) *adv.*
  to the whole quantity or extent
    Synonyms: totally, completely, entirely

No precaution could have been more **obvious** than our **refraining** from communication with Magwitch that day, yet this made me more worried. I started at every footstep and every sound, believing that he was discovered and taken and that the footsteps were those of a messenger who would tell me so.

The fateful morning was dawning when I looked out the window. The winking lights upon the bridges were already pale, the coming sun was like a marsh of fire on the horizon. Bridges, turning coldly gray, with only a touch of light from the sky, **spanned** the river, which was still dark and mysterious.

It was one of those March days when the sun shines hot and the wind blows cold, when it is summer in the light and winter in the shade. Herbert, Startop, and I had our coats with us, and I took a bag. I took no more than what filled one bag. Where I might go, what I might do, or when I might return, were questions **utterly** unknown to me. Nor did I worry my mind with them, for it was **wholly** set on Magwitch's safety. I only

LOITER (<u>loi</u> ter) *v.* **-ing**, **-ed**
  to stand around as if you have nothing to do
    Synonyms: hang around, dawdle

HAIL (hayl) *v.* **-ing**, **-ed**
  to call, to try to be noticed by shouting
    Synonyms: signal, flag down

DISTINGUISHING (diss <u>ting</u> gwish ing) *adj.*
  serving to identify a species, group, or
  individual
    Synonyms: distinctive, differentiating

BRISKLY (<u>brisk</u> lee) *adv.*
  with a rapid motion
    Synonyms: quickly, speedily, eagerly

wondered, for a moment, under what circumstances I should next see those old rooms, if ever.

For a moment, before we entered the boat, we **loitered** at the bottom of the stairs, as if we had not quite decided to go upon the water at all. Of course, I had taken care that the boat should be ready. The tide would be with us for some time. The ship for Hamburg as well as a ship bound for Rotterdam, Netherlands, would both leave from London that morning. We knew at what time to expect them, and would **hail** the first one. That way, if by any accident we were not taken aboard by the first ship, we should have another chance. We knew the **distinguishing** marks of each vessel.

We were finally escaping, and it made us all very relieved and very scared.

Early as it was, there were plenty of <u>barges</u> out on the water and we went ahead, pulling up our oars and dipping them back into the water **briskly**. We were certain we had not been followed by any boat. And then I, with a beating heart, saw the Mill Pond stairs where

COMPOSED (kuhm <u>pozd</u>) *adv.*
  in a calm way
    Synonyms: self-possessed, serene

DISMAL (<u>diz</u> muhl) *adj.*
  causing or having gloom and depression
    Synonyms: sad, horrible, dull

RIPPLE (rip puhl) *n.*
  a small wave
    Synonyms: pulse, swell

Magwitch was to meet us, and there he was. We touched the stairs, and he was on board and we were off.

"Dear boy!" Magwitch said, putting his arm on my shoulder, as he took his seat in the boat. "Dear boy, well done. Thank 'ee, thank 'ee!"

"If all goes well," said I, "you will be free and safe again within a few hours."

"Well," he said, drawing a long breath, "I hope so." He sat as **composed** and contented as if we were already out of England.

Quickly, we dipped our oars into the water and set out. We rowed strongly at first, not tiring. Then, as time and work wore on, we slowed. But still we rowed on.

At this **dismal** time we began to worry that we were followed. Sometimes, one of us would say in a low voice, "What was that **ripple**?" Or another would say, "Is that a boat over there?" Afterwards we would fall into silence, and I would sit impatiently thinking about what an unusual amount of noise the oars made.

We could suddenly see a stretch of shore. I

CLOAK (klohk) *n.*
a loose-fitting piece of outer clothing
Synonyms: coat, mantle

SHRINK (shrink) *v.* **-ing, shrunk**
to become smaller
Synonyms: diminish, contract, decrease

called to Herbert and Startop to row carefully so that the steamer might see us waiting for her. I begged Magwitch to sit quite still, wrapped in his **cloak**. He answered cheerily, "Trust to me, dear boy," and sat like a statue.

Meantime, we saw two steamers pulling up towards us, coming full speed, so I got the bags ready. But just then, a four-oared rowboat shot out and began moving alongside us, leaving just room enough for the movement of the oars. She drifted when we drifted, and the four rowers pulled a stroke or two when we pulled. Of the two passengers sitting in the other boat, one steered the boat and looked at us attentively. The other passenger was wrapped up much as Magwitch was. When he looked at us, he seemed to **shrink**, and then he whispered some instruction to the man steering the boat.

Startop could make out, after a few minutes, which steamer was first, and, in a low voice, said, "Hamburg." The steamer was coming near us very fast. The beating of her paddles grew louder and louder. I felt as if her shadow were absolutely

APPREHEND (ap ri <u>hend</u>) *v.* **-ing**, **-ed**
to take into custody
Synonyms: arrest, capture

FRANTICALLY (<u>fran</u> tik uh lee) *adv.*
in an excited way
Synonyms: wildly, madly

upon us. Then, suddenly, a voice from the other rowboat hailed us.

"You have a convict there," cried the voice. "That's the man, wrapped in the cloak. His name is Abel Magwitch. I **apprehend** that man, and call upon him to surrender, and I demand you to assist."

At the same moment, he steered his boat in front of us. His rowers had a firm grip on our boat before we knew what they were doing. All this activity caused great confusion on board the steamer that had been coming toward us. I heard people on board calling to us, and I heard the order given to stop the paddles, and I heard them stop. In the same moment, I saw the man who had been steering the other rowboat reach across and lay his hand on Magwitch's shoulder. Suddenly, Magwitch stood up, pulling the cloak from off the face of the shrinking sitter in the boat. Both rowboats were swinging round with the force of the tide, and all the men on board the steamer were running forward quite **frantically**. At the same time, I saw the face of the man in the other rowboat. It was the face

FURIOUS (<u>fyur</u> ee uhss) *adj.*
1. characterized by anger
2. full of energy or activity
    Synonyms: fierce, violent

of the other convict of long ago! Compeyson! His face tilted backward with a terror on it that I shall never forget. Then I heard a great cry on board the steamer and a loud splash in the water, and I felt our boat sink from under me.

It was but for an instant that I seemed to struggle in the waters. That instant passed, and I was taken on board the other rowboat. Herbert was already there, and Startop was there, too. But our boat was gone, and the two convicts were gone as well.

What with the cries aboard the steamer, and the **furious** blowing of her steam, and the way all the boats kept moving, I could not at first tell sky from water. But the crew of the other rowboat righted it with great speed. Soon, a dark object was seen in the water, coming towards us. No one spoke, but the man steering the boat held up his hand, and kept the boat straight. As the object came nearer, I saw it to be Magwitch, swimming. He was taken on board and put in chains.

The rowboat was kept steady, and a silent lookout for Compeyson was begun. But

CAPSIZE (<u>kap</u> size) *v.* **-ing, -ed**
   to turn upside down
      Synonyms: overturn, invert

PURCHASE (<u>pur</u> chuhss) *v.* **-ing, -ed**
   to pay for something
      Synonyms: buy, acquire

everybody knew that it was hopeless for both our escape and for Compeyson.

At length we gave up the search and pulled to shore. We went to a tavern where I was able to get some comforts for Magwitch, who had received a bad injury in the chest and a deep cut in the head.

The injury to his chest, which he had received against the side of the other rowboat, made his breathing extremely painful. He added that he could not say what might or might not have happened to Compeyson. When he had pulled back Compeyson's cloak to identity him, they had both gone overboard together, and our boat had **capsized**. He told me in a whisper that they had gone down fiercely locked in each other's arms. There had been a struggle under water, and he had freed himself and swum away.

I asked the officer's permission to **purchase** any spare clothing I could get at the tavern in order to change the prisoner's wet clothes. He gave it readily.

Compeyson was now thought to be drowned.

AFFECTIONATELY (uh <u>fek</u> shuh nuht lee) *adv.*
with great feeling and loving emotion
Synonyms: fondly, tenderly

CONSTANCY (<u>kon</u> stuhn see) *n.*
the act of being steady of purpose, not changing
Synonyms: regularity, dependability

SERIES (<u>sihr</u> eez) *n.*
a number of objects coming one after another
Synonyms: group, row, arrangement

A search was made for his body where it was likeliest to come ashore.

My bad feelings toward Magwitch had all melted away. In the hunted, wounded, creature who held my hand in his, I only saw a man who had meant to be my benefactor and who had felt **affectionately**, gratefully, and generously towards me with great **constancy** through a **series** of years. I only saw in him a much better man than I had been to Joe.

His breathing became more painful as the night drew on, and often he groaned. I could not hope that he would be fairly treated. He had been presented in the worst light at his trial long ago. He had been in prison. He had returned to me under a life sentence and he had caused the death of the man who was the cause of his arrest.

As we returned towards the setting sun, I told him how grieved I was to think that he had come home for me.

"Dear boy," he answered, smiling, "I'm content to take my chance. I've seen my boy be a

OTHERWISE (<u>uhth</u> ur wize) *adv.*
in a different way
Synonyms: alternatively, differently

ENRICHING (en <u>rich</u> ing) *n.*
the act of making someone rich or giving them money
Synonym: benefitting

PERISH (<u>per</u> ished) *v.* **-ing**, **-ed**
to end forever
Synonyms: die, collapse, expire

gentleman. But it's best, too, that a gentleman should not be associated with me now.

"I will never stir from your side," said, "I will be as true to you as you have been to me!"

I felt his hand tremble as it held mine. He turned his face away, and I heard that old sound in his throat, softened now, like all the rest of him. It was a good thing that he had touched this point, for it put into my mind what I might not **otherwise** have thought of until too late, that he need never know how his hopes of **enriching** me had **perished**.

IDENTIFY (eye <u>den</u> tuh fye) *v.* **-ing, -ed**
   to tell one's identity, to establish who someone is
      Synonyms: recognize, label, describe

ARRIVAL (uh <u>rye</u> vuhl) *n.*
   the act of arriving or coming to a place
      Synonyms: landing, entrance, appearance

RETAIN (ri <u>tayne</u>) *v.* **-ing, -ed**
   to maintain possession
      Synonyms: keep, hold, withhold

CHAPTER 13

Magwitch was taken to Police Court next day. He would have been immediately taken for trial, but it was necessary to send down for an old officer of the prison-ship to **identify** him for certain. Nobody doubted that Compeyson was on the tides, dead.

I had gone directly to Mr. Jaggers at his private house, on my **arrival** overnight, to **retain** his help. Mr. Jaggers on the prisoner's behalf, would admit nothing. He told me, however, that once

OBTAIN (uhb <u>tayn</u>) *v.* **-ing**, **-ed**
    to gain possession of something
        Synonyms: get, gain, acquire, procure

ACCURATE (<u>ak</u> yuh ruht) *adj.*
    exactly correct, without error
        Synonyms: precise, definite

DESIGNATION (dez ig <u>nay</u> shuhn) *n.*
    the act of marking or pointing out something
        Synonyms: description, identification

the officer identified Magwitch, the case would be over in five minutes, and no power on earth could prevent it going against us.

I told Mr. Jaggers I wanted to keep Magwitch ignorant of how I had spent his wealth. Mr. Jaggers was angry with me for having "let it slip through my fingers."

There appeared to be reason for supposing that the drowned Compeyson had hoped for a reward. He had **obtained** some **accurate** knowledge of Magwitch's affairs. When his body was found, many miles from the scene of his death, notes were found, too, folded in a case he carried. Among these were the name of a bank in New South Wales, where a sum of money was, and the **designation** of certain lands of value. Both these pieces of information were in a list that Magwitch had recently given to Mr. Jaggers.

I was sad and could think of nothing else except for Magwitch's trial, which would be in a month. But Herbert, looking ahead, worried for my future. "My dear fellow," said Herbert, "Have you thought ahead at all?"

EXPAND (ek <u>spand</u>) *v.*
    to increase in size or importance
        Synonyms: grow, enlarge, develop

PREOCCUPIED (pree <u>ok</u> yuh pyde) *adj.*
    absorbed or lost in thought
        Synonyms: distracted, engrossed

INFIRMARY (in <u>fur</u> mur ee) *n.*
    a place for the treatment of the ill, injured, or
    weak, especially in an institution such as a
    school, prison, or military unit
        Synonyms: hospital, dispensary

"I have been afraid to think of any future."

"In the place where I work, we need a—"

I saw that his delicacy was avoiding the right word, so I said, "A clerk."

"A clerk. And I hope it is not at all unlikely that he may **expand**, as I have, into a partner. Now, will you come to me?"

"I soon will have a wife," Herbert pursued, "and if you will live with us after we marry, I am sure that she will do her best to make you happy."

I thanked him, but said I could not yet make sure of joining him as he so kindly offered. I was too **preoccupied** with Magwitch.

When I next visited Magwitch in prison, I saw he was very ill. He had broken two ribs, and he breathed with great pain and difficulty, which increased daily. He spoke very little. But he was ever ready to listen to me. It became the first duty of my life to say to him, and read to him, what I knew he ought to hear.

Being far too ill to remain in the prison, he was removed into the **infirmary**. This gave me

INDUSTRIOUS (in <u>duhss</u> tree us) *adj.*
eager at work, school, or other activities
Synonyms: hard-working, diligent,
conscientious, productive

PETITION (puh <u>tish</u> uhn) *n.*
a formal request for action by an authority
Synonym: appeal

chances of being with him that I could not other-wise have had.

The trial came on, and, when Magwitch was taken to court, he was seated in a chair.No objection was made to my getting close to him.

The trial was very short. Such things as could be said for him were said – how he had taken to **industrious** habits and had done well lawfully. But still, he had returned, and because of that, he was found guilty and he must die. His money and property, too, were doomed – taken by the Crown

I began that night to write out a **petition** to the government, setting down what I knew about Magwitch, and telling how he had come back for me. When I had finished it and sent it in, I wrote out other petitions to such men in authority as I hoped were the most merciful.

The daily visits I could make were short-ened now.

"You always waits at the gate, don't you, dear boy?" he asked.

"Yes. Not to lose a moment of the time."

PRESSURE (<u>presh</u> ur) *n.*
the feeling of being pressed or touched, the act of pressing something
Synonyms: force, push, weight

EFFORT (<u>ef</u> urt) *n.*
the use of physical or mental energy
Synonyms: strain, struggle

BITTER (<u>bit</u> tur) *adj.*
1. having a sharp, unpleasant taste
2. causing an unpleasant, painful sensation
Synonyms: harsh, stinging, biting

"Thank 'ee dear boy, thank 'ee. God bless you! You've never deserted me, dear boy."

I pressed his hand in silence, for I could not forget that I had once meant to desert him.

"And what's the best of all," he said, "you've been more comfortable with me, since I was under a dark cloud, than when the sun shone. That's best of all."

"Dear Magwitch, I must tell you something. Do you understand what I say?"

A gentle **pressure** on my hand.

"You had a child once, whom you loved and lost."

A stronger pressure on my hand.

"She lived and found powerful friends. She is living now. She is a lady and very beautiful. And I love her!"

With a last **effort**, he raised my hand to his lips. Then he gently let it sink upon his breast again. His head dropped quietly on his breast and he was gone from me, and I wept long and **bitter** tears for him, and for myself, for I would dearly miss him.

FEVER (<u>fee</u> vur) *n.*
 a body temperature greater than 98.6 degrees
  Synonym: raised temperature

CONSISTENT (kuhn <u>siss</u> tuhnt) *adj.*
 always behaving in the same way
  Synonyms: reliable, steady

I was left to myself. For a day or two, I lay on the sofa or on the floor, anywhere I happened to sink down, with a heavy heart.

I had a **fever**, I suffered greatly. I often lost my mind and thought I saw, in the great chair at the bedside, one **consistent** feature, which was Joe. What seemed like weeks later, I opened my eyes, and still I saw Joe.

I took courage and said "Is it Joe?"

And dear old Joe answered, "Yes, old friend."

"Oh Joe, you break my heart! Look angry at me, Joe. Don't be so good to me, for I have not been so good to you!"

Joe rested his head down on the pillow at my side, and put his arm round my neck, in his joy that I knew him.

Joe's eyes were red, but I was holding his hand, and we both felt happy.

"How long have I been here, ill, dear Joe?"

"A long time. It's the end of May, Pip. Tomorrow is the first of June."

"And have you been here all that time, Joe?"

"Pretty much, old chap. When the news of

INTRUDE (in <u>trood</u>) *v.* **-ing**, **-ed**
  to force one's way in without being invited
  Synonyms: barge in, infringe

VAINLY (<u>vayn</u> lee) *adv.*
  without a chance of success
  Synonyms: hopelessly, futilely, fruitlessl

your being ill were brought by letter, Biddy said 'Go to him, without loss of time.'"

"Miss Havisham, has she recovered?" I asked, and Joe shook his head sadly.

"What becomes of her property?"

"Miss Estella has it," said Joe.

Sick again, feverish, I was like a child in Joe's hands. He would sit and talk to me as he had in the old days. We looked forward to the day when I should go out for a ride, as we had once looked forward to the day of my apprenticeship. I felt that I was not nearly thankful enough, that I was too weak.

But get better I did, and one morning I woke to find a note, written in Joe's hand, and I could only imagine that Biddy must have taught him.

"Not wishful to **intrude** I have left. You are well again dear Pip and will do better without JO. P.S. Ever the best of friends."

Enclosed in the letter was a receipt for my costs. Down to that moment, I had **vainly** thought that my creditors had withdrawn until I should be quite recovered. I had never dreamed of Joe's

RELIEVE (ri <u>leev</u>) *v.* **-ing, -ed**
to lessen, to give assistance
Synonyms: improve, lighten, alleviate, help

HUMBLY (<u>huhm</u> blee) *adv.*
without pride
Synonyms: modestly, meekly, courteously

having paid the money. But Joe had paid it, and the receipt was in his name.

What remained for me now was to follow him to the old forge, to tell him everything, to ask forgiveness and to **relieve** my mind and heart.

I also thought that I would go to Biddy, that I would show her how **humbly** I came back. I would tell her how I had lost all I once hoped for, that I would remind her of our old confidences. Then I would ask her to marry me and ask if I should work at the forge with Joe or try for a different occupation.

FATIGUE (fuh <u>teeg</u>) *n.*
the state of being physically or mentally tired
Synonyms: weariness, exhaustion, tiredness

BELLOWS (<u>bell</u> ohz) *n.*
an instrument for moving air, especially to
a fire
Synonym: pump

CHAPTER 14

It was evening when I arrived, feeling **fatigue** from the journey I had so often made so easily.

The forge was a very short distance off, and I went towards it, listening for the clink of Joe's hammer. All was still. I saw that it was closed. No gleam of fire, no glittering shower of sparks, no roar of **bellows**.

But the house was not deserted, and the best parlor seemed to be in use, for there were white

EMBRACE (em <u>brayss</u>) *n.*
the holding of someone or something in one's arms
Synonyms: clasp, hug

RESTORING (ri <u>stor</u> ing) *adj.*
bringing back to the original condition
Synonym: healing, reviving, curing

BAFFLED (<u>baf</u> uhld) *adj.*
unsure or frustrated
Synonyms: puzzled, confused

curtains fluttering in its window. I went softly towards it, meaning to peep in, when Joe and Biddy stood before me, arm in arm.

At first Biddy gave a cry, as if she thought it was my ghost. But in another moment she was in my **embrace**. We wept to see each other. I wept because she looked so fresh and pleasant. She wept because I looked so worn.

"It's my wedding-day!" cried Biddy, in a burst of happiness, "and I am married to Joe!"

They had taken me into the kitchen, and I had laid my head down on the old table. Biddy held one of my hands to her lips, and Joe's **restoring** touch was on my shoulder. "I would have told you, but you warn't strong enough, my boy, fur to be surprised," said Joe.

They were both overjoyed to see me and delighted that I should have come by accident to make their day complete!

My first thought was one of great thankfulness that I had never breathed my last **baffled** hope of marrying Biddy to Joe. Better that he never have his happiness shadowed by pity for me.

REPAY (ri <u>pay</u>) *v.* **-ing**, **ed**
to give back, to pay back
Synonyms: return, compensate, make
restitution

"Dear Biddy," said I, "you have the best husband in the whole world."

"And, dear Joe, you have the best wife in the whole world!"

Joe looked at me with a quivering lip and put his sleeve before his eyes.

"I am soon going abroad, and I shall never rest until I have worked for the money which you have given me and have sent it to you. I wish, dear Joe and Biddy, that I could **repay** all that I owe you a thousand times over!"

They were both melted by these words, and both begged me to say no more.

"And now, though I know you have already done it in your own kind hearts, pray tell me, both, that you forgive me!"

"Oh, dear old Pip, old chap," said Joe. "I forgive you, if I have anythink to forgive!"

"Amen! And so do I!" echoed Biddy.

I left Joe and Biddy and then I sold all I had, and put aside as much as I could, for my creditors, who gave me ample time to pay them in full. Then I went out and joined Herbert. Within a

RESPONSIBILITY (ri spon suh <u>bil</u> uh tee) *n.*
1. something for which one is in charge
   Synonyms: task, care, burden
2. the state of being trustworthy
   Synonym: dependability

FRUGALLY (<u>froo</u> guhl lee) *adj.*
trying not to waste money or goods
   Synonyms: thriftily, economically

CORRESPONDENCE (kor uh <u>spon</u> duhnss) *n.*
communication, usually by written letters
   Synonyms: mail, messages

month, I had left England, and within two months I was working overseas as a clerk to Clarriker and Co., and within four months I was given more **responsibility**.

Many a year went round before I was a partner in the company. But I lived happily and **frugally**, paid my debts, and maintained a constant **correspondence** with Biddy and Joe. I never made tons of money. We were not in a grand way of business. But we had a good name, and worked for our money, and did very well.

STOOL (stool) *n.*
a seat with no back or arms
Synonym: chair

CHAPTER 15

For eleven years, I had not seen Joe nor Biddy, though they had both been often in my thoughts. But on an evening one December, I laid my hand on the latch of the kitchen door. There, as strong as ever, though a little gray, sat Joe, and there, sitting on my own little **stool** looking at the fire, was I again!

"We giv' him the name of Pip for your sake, dear old chap," said Joe, delighted, when I took

SITE (site) *n.*
the place or setting of something
Synonyms: location, point, scene

SEPARATE (<u>sep</u> uh rate) *v.* **-ing, ed**
to set or keep apart; in this context, to live
apart
Synonyms: divide, disconnect

CRUELTY (<u>krool</u> tee) *n.*
a deliberate unkindness, an act that causes pain
or suffering
Synonyms: viciousness, brutality, meanness

AJAR (uh <u>jar</u>) *adj.*
open slightly
Synonyms: unclosed, unlatched

another stool by the child's side. "We hoped he might grow a little bit like you, and we think he do."

Said Biddy, gently watching me with the child. "You must marry."

"I am already quite an old <u>bachelor</u>."

"Dear Pip," said Biddy, "have you quite forgotten her?"

I shook my head, for I knew that I intended to revisit the **site** of the old house that evening.

I had heard Estella had been leading a most unhappy life and had **separated** from her husband, who had used her with great **cruelty**. And I had heard of the death of her husband, from an accident on a horse, two years before. For all I knew, she was married again.

I came to the house but there was none now, just the wall of the old garden. A gate in the fence was standing **ajar**. I pushed it open and went in.

A cold mist had veiled the afternoon. But, the stars were shining beyond the mist, and the evening was not dark. I beheld a figure and cried out, "Estella!"

MAJESTY (<u>madj</u> juss tee) *n.*

the dignity or other qualities associated with a king or queen

Synonyms: splendor, magnificence

CHARM (charm) *n.*

the power to please or delight

Synonyms: appeal, attractiveness, magic

"I am greatly changed. I wonder how you still know me."

The freshness of her beauty was indeed gone, but its **majesty** and its **charm** remained. We sat down on a bench that was near,

"I have very often intended to come back, but have been prevented by many circumstances. Poor, poor old place. The ground belongs to me. It is the only possession I have not lost. Everything else has gone from me, little by little, but I have kept this.

"Is it to be built on?"

"At last, it is. I came here to take leave of it before its change. And you," she said, in a voice of touching interest, "You live abroad still?"

"Still."

"And do well, I am sure?"

"I work pretty hard for my living, and there-fore – yes, I do well."

"I have often thought of you," said Estella.

"You have always held your place in my heart," I answered.

And we were silent again until she spoke.

"You said to me," returned Estella, very

EARNESTLY (<u>urn</u> ist lee) *adv.*
in a serious and honest way
Synonym: eagerly

CONSIDERATE (kuhn <u>sid</u> uh rit) *adj.*
thinking of someone else's feelings
Synonym: kind

earnestly, 'Bless you, God forgive you!' Can you say that to me now when my suffering has taught me to understand what yours must have been? I have been bent and broken, but I hope into a better shape. Be as **considerate** and good to me as you were, and tell me we are friends."

"We are friends," said I, rising and bending over her, as she rose from the bench.

"And will continue friends," said Estella.

I took her hand in mine, and we went out of the ruined place. And, as the morning mists had risen long ago when I first left the forge, so the evening mists were rising now. And in all the broad expanse of light they showed to me, I saw no shadow of another separation from her.

RESOURCES

GLOSSARY

The following are words and terms that you are not
likely to be tested on, but understanding them may
enhance your appreciation of the text.

apprenticeship (uh <u>pren</u> tiss ship) *n.*
> a system in which a young person learned a
> trade or craft from a master; apprentices worked
> for low wages, often for just room and board.
> After their time of apprenticeship was up,
> however, apprentices had learned a craft or trade
> that allowed them to earn a living.

bank note *n.*
> a note issued by a bank promising to pay the
> owner a certain amount

barge (barj) *n.*
> a long boat with a flat bottom towed or pulled
> by another boat; bargemen work on barges

bachelor (<u>bach</u> uh lur) *n.*
> an unmarried man

beggar my neighbor *idiom*
a simple card game for children in which players "buy" face cards with the other cards in the deck

blacksmith (<u>blak</u> smith) *n.*
someone who makes horseshoes and works with iron

constable (<u>kon</u> stuh bul) *n.*
a police officer

creditor (<u>kred</u> it or) *n.*
a person to whom money is owed

forge (forj) *n.*
a furnace or fireplace where metal is shaped by being heated and then hammered

grave clothes *n.*
the clothes someone is buried in

Hulks (hulkz) *n.*
prison ships

knaves (nayves) *n.*
the jacks in a deck of cards

laid waste *v.*
to allow to become messy and dirty

mincemeat (minss meet) *n.*
a mixture of apples, raisins, and meat that is
used to fill a pie

one-pound note *idiom*
paper money worth about $10 in Dickens's day

sent for life *idiom*
sentenced to a lifetime in exile or prison

steamer (<u>steem</u> er) *n.*
an ocean ship powered by steam

shutter (shuht ur) *n.*
a moveable cover for a window that shuts out
light and weather, usually arranged in pairs

surgeon (<u>sur</u> juhn) *n.*
a medical professional who carries out operations or physical cures

Thames (tems) *n.*
river that passes through the city of London, England

warmint (<u>whar</u> mint) *n.*
a mispronounciation of *varmint,* a troublesome animal

wheelwright (<u>wheel</u> rite) *n.*
someone who makes or repairs wheels

wittles (<u>wit</u> tuhls) *n.*
a mispronunciation of *vittles,* nourishment

BOOK REPORT

Students are often asked to write book reports about the books they read. The key to writing a good report is to organize your ideas before you start writing. Use the following questions to organize your ideas for a book report about *Great Expectations.*

1. What is the title?

2. Who is the author? What do you know about him?

3. When and where does the story take place?

4. Who is the main character of the book?

5. What happens to this person during the story? What is this person like at the beginning? And at the end? What problems does this person face? How does this person solve them?

6. Who are the other important characters? What are they like? What happens to them?

7. What do you think is the main theme or idea of the book?

8. What is the main thing you learned from this book?

9. What would you tell a friend about this book if he or she asked you about it?

DISCUSSION QUESTIONS

Here are several questions to think about and to discuss with classmates, friends, and other people who have read Dickens's *Great Expectations.*

1. Pip's story is very much the story of his dream that he will, some day, be a "gentleman." What does being a gentleman mean to him? Why is it so important to him? Do you think he becomes a gentleman at the end of the book?

2. As the novel goes on, Pip's feelings toward Joe Gargery and Magwitch undergo several changes. What changes do you see in these feelings? What do these changes tell you about changes in Pip's own character?

3. Pip is not the only character who undergoes changes in the book. How does Estella change? How does Miss Havisham change?

4. The world in which Pip lives is one with a strict social order. What social classes do you see at work in this society? How do they affect the people of the novel? How do you think Dickens felt about that social system?

5. Pip's love for Estella is one of the main themes of the book. Do you think *Great Expectations* is a love story? Why or why not?

6. It has been said that, in the England of Dickens's time, life was good if you were rich but harsh if you were poor. Judging from *Great Expectations,* do you agree or disagree with this statement. Use examples from the book to support your view.